THE HALF MAN

a novel by
Anne Billson

By the same author:

Novels:
Dream Demon (a novelisation)
Suckers
Stiff Lips
The Ex
The Coming Thing

Non-Fiction:
Screen Lovers
My Name is Michael Caine
The Thing (BFI Modern Classics)
Buffy the Vampire Slayer (BFI TV Classics)
Let The Right One In (Devil's Advocates)
Cats on Film

e-books:
Billson Film Database
Spoilers Part 1
Spoilers Part 2
Breast Man: A Conversation with Russ Meyer

Copyright © 2019 Anne Billson

All rights reserved. No part of this publication may be reproduced in any material form (including photocopying or storing in any medium by electronic means and whether or not transiently or incidentally to some other use of this publication) without the permission of the copyright owner.

ISBN-13: 978-1718632936
ISBN-10: 1718632932

THE HALF MAN

PROLOGUE: 1938

For six centuries, Castle Pretorius had lain seven leagues south-west of Prague. Over the years its owners and occupants had tried to bend its wayward character to their will by imposing additions and alterations of their own, but without success. The embellishments were plain to see - unnecessary wings and clashing turrets, windows that didn't match, pointless outbreaks of ostentatious bas relief, mysterious arches which, to the uninitiated, led nowhere. It was an architectural ragbag full of unexpected microclimates, sudden gales and pockets of unsavoury warmth, and no-one knew how many skeletons had been entombed within the walls.

Inside, the disharmony was harder to discern with the naked eye, but the instant you stepped over the threshold you could feel it in your bones. If only those salons and ballrooms, staircases and passageways, sculleries and kitchens, bedrooms and dungeons (especially the dungeons) had been able to speak of the horrors they had witnessed through the ages, you would have blocked your ears and begged them to shut up.

By the end of World War Two those stones would be engraved with a fresh agglomeration of atrocities, but on Sunday the ninth of October, 1938, these were still just a gleam in the eyes of some of the high-ranking officers in black dress uniforms and swastika armbands stepping out of the chauffeur-driven Mercedes and Daimlers lining the wide gravel driveway. Clinging to their arms were perfumed women in furs and jewels; festering in their hearts were twisted secrets and unimaginable cruelty.

There were men in tuxedos too, for this was not an exclusively military affair, but a social gathering, designed to seduce, not intimidate. Trapezoids of light spilled on to the terrace from the nineteenth century French windows incongruously embedded in the ground floor, accompanied by drunken laughter, the tinkling of crystal glassware, and the sophisticated syncopations of Willi Engl and his Orchestra.

Far above the ground floor activity, the gothic turrets and spires of the castle stood black and immutable against the moon. The upper levels were in darkness... except for an arrowslit near the summit of one of the highest towers, within which a hypothetical observer standing with binoculars on the lawn below might have been able to discern a faint flickering.

The source of the flickering was a candle flame. Inside the tower, it cast its wavering yellow glow across the faces of two men and one woman. They were formally dressed, like the revellers below, but their furtive demeanour indicated they had purposely strayed from the throng into a part of the castle off limits to visitors. And no part of it more off limits than this cramped library lined with dark wood panelling, and bookshelves creaking beneath the weight of crumbling volumes and stacks of ancient scrolls.

Quentin 'Tiger' Steele, oldest of the three conspirators, was running his hands over the wood panelling, and counting under his breath. 'Forty-seven. Forty-eight. Forty-nine... Yes, this must be the place.' At the touch of his fingers, one of the panels slid noiselessly to one side, disclosing a small dark niche.

'Well done, daddy!' said the young woman holding the candle and peering over her father's shoulder with a look of fierce determination and intelligence that belied her extreme youth. Her name was Araminta 'Minty' Steele. At her side was her fiancé, Justin Saxby, her senior by only a couple of years. They were a well-matched couple, both of them on the cusp of adulthood, their no-nonsense bond forged in warm friendship and shared adventure rather than any mushy romantic sentiment.

As the three interlopers craned their necks to see what the niche might contain, Justin felt unevenness beneath his feet. He kicked aside a corner of the oriental rug, exposing a semi-circle of runic symbols carved into the parquet.

He frowned down at the sight and tugged at Steele's sleeve. 'Watch your step, sir.'

Steele sank into a crouch to examine the semi-circle at closer quarters, tracing the symbols with his fingers and muttering something under his breath before straightening up again with a troubled expression.

'We won't be harmed by this. It's not *us* he's afraid of.'

'Are you sure he didn't see us downstairs?' Minty asked. 'He's just the sort of sneaky old cove who would lure us into a trap.'

Steele smiled grimly. 'Too busy licking the boots of his friends from the Schutzstaffel. There are some clay tablets in the Jewish Museum he would dearly love to get his hands on, and he probably thinks if he plies his new chums with enough champagne they'll agree to a trade. I know him.'

'And *he* knows *you*, don't forget.'

'He *thinks* he does, my darling, but if he really did know me he would never have double-crossed me in the first place. Bring that candle nearer, please.'

Minty moved the candle closer to the niche. The three of them put their heads together to peer inside. The flame lit up a filigree casket the size of a shoebox, which in turn dappled their faces with reflected gold.

Justin let out a low whistle. 'Got to hand it to you, sir. Thought it was just a legend.'

Steele chuckled. 'When you reach my age, my boy, you realise that even the most fanciful legends contain nuggets of truth.'

The light was so dim and volatile that not one of the three noticed the golden filigree shifting slightly.

Steele readied himself to reach in and grasp the casket, but at the last moment hesitated.

'I don't like it. It's too easy.'

The crash of breaking glass and a burst of hysterical laughter from the terrace below made the three of them jump guiltily.

'Hurry up, daddy,' said Minty. 'Let's grab it and scarper before someone starts wondering where we got to.'

Steele suppressed his forebodings and reached into the niche. At the very instant that his fingers touched the casket, a small section of filigree uncoiled from it and struck. Steele yelped in surprise and snatched his arm back. Clamped to his wrist were the fanged jaws of a tiny golden snake, not much bigger than a garden worm. Its tail whipped back and forth as it injected its venom into his bloodstream.

Without stopping to think, Justin yanked the creature from Steele's wrist, hurled it to the ground and crushed it beneath his heel. When, cautiously, he lifted his foot, all that remained was a glittering golden powder which almost immediately scattered into the air, like the dying sparks of a spent firework.

No sooner had the last glimmer faded into nothingness than a commotion erupted somewhere far below their feet: feet running hither and thither, accompanied by bellowing and the slamming of doors.

'We're rumbled!' said Minty.

Justin snatched the candle from her grasp and held the flame to the edge of the heavy damask curtains. The fabric began to scorch and smoulder. The room filled with the smell of burning.

'Minty!' said Justin. 'The casket!'

'Be careful,' said Steele. He clutched his wrist, which was already beginning to swell up.

Minty hesitated for only a second before reaching into the niche and pulling the casket towards her. It was heavier than she'd expected, but she managed to draw it all the way out without further mishap.

'Quick!' said Justin, heading for the door. But Steele, instead of following, turned to one of the shelves and tilted his head to read the titles of the books on it.

'Daddy, please, there's no time for that!'

'Sir!' said Justin.

Steele grasped the spine of one of the leather tomes and jerked it towards him. There was a click, and the shelf slid to one side. Behind was another dark space, this one roughly the height and breadth of a man.

'I knew it!' said Steele. 'This way!'

Justin and Minty exchanged a fearful glance, but didn't need telling twice. Still holding the candle, Justin took a deep breath and dove fearlessly into the darkness.

9

Minty stepped in after him with the casket, and Steele followed, pulling the secret door shut behind them.

The passageway was so narrow they were obliged to proceed in single file. Justin led the way, head down as he shouldered through dusty shrouds of clinging cobwebs.

'Just as well I swotted up on the history of this place,' said Steele. 'Such a honeycomb of hidden rooms and corridors that I doubt even our degenerate friend has managed to uncover them all.'

Justin breached another cobweb curtain. 'Hope you don't mind spiders, Minty.'

'I love spiders!' said Minty. 'I just hope there aren't any more snakes.'

'Only snakes we're likely to find around here are occult simulacri,' said Justin. 'All right back there, sir?'

'I'm fine,' said Steele. His voice was steady, but, unseen by his companions, he gritted his teeth in pain. Droplets of perspiration were breaking out on his brow.

'Where does this lead, sir?' asked Justin.

Steele forced a chuckle. 'I have no idea. Let us just hope it doesn't spit us out into the ballroom right in front of those mutton-headed stooges.'

They followed the passageway for a few more minutes until the flickering candlelight allowed them to discern the top of a stone staircase spiralling down into darkness.

'Here we go!' said Justin. 'Watch where you put your feet!'

He began to feel his way down the uneven stone steps, testing his footing on each of the treads, which were scarcely wide enough for the average male foot. Minty and Steele followed carefully. The steps wound

10

downwards for so long, and so unrelentingly, that their heads began to swim, but finally, after what seemed like an eternity, the ground levelled out and they found themselves at the beginning of another passageway. This one was wider, but the sloping floor was strewn with treacherous rubble, and the air reeked of damp and decay.

The further they went, the colder it became, until their breath lingered in the semi-darkness like silvery clouds. Minty's bare arms, wrapped tightly around the casket, were covered in goose-pimples and mottled with red marks from where the sharp edges of the ornamentation had been digging into her skin. Justin held on to the candle until the guttering flame scorched his fingers and he had to discard the stub, leaving them in darkness punctured only by a miniscule pinprick of greenish light far up ahead. The corridor was playing tricks with perspective, so that it was impossible to tell if the pinprick was somewhere close, or many miles away.

'The light at the end of the tunnel!' said Justin, sounding more jovial than he felt. He just hoped they weren't trapped in one of the Perpetual Passageways he'd read about, but he knew better than to express this fear out loud. Fear could be contagious, he knew, and in itself was capable of conjuring chimeras out of the empty air, especially in an evil place like this.

After that, they stopped talking and concentrated on keeping their footing - especially Minty, hampered by the satin shoes that had so perfectly complemented her ballgown, but which had not been designed for clambering over debris. But eventually the scree gave way to larger, flatter slabs of rock and thence to tightly-packed earth, which made their progress easier.

At last they arrived at a door. A dim green glow leaked out through the cracks in its frame. 'Let's hope it isn't locked,' said Justin, his hand on the doorknob, and on his face a look of determination that suggested he was prepared to break the door down with brute force, should it prove necessary.

But it wasn't necessary. The door opened with only a token creak of reluctance, and they stepped over the threshold into a dimly lit room with green-painted curved walls, into one of which was set another door. Much to their relief, this one let them out into the cool night air, and part of a formally landscaped garden. They looked around, trying to get their bearings, and saw they had emerged from a small gatehouse. A long way behind them, the upper windows of Castle Pretorius were lit by flames. Plumes of smoke drifted lazily across the face of the moon. They could hear shouting, and the clank of buckets, and the distant murmuring from a knot of people clustered on the lawn, faces tipped up to gaze at the burning tower. Someone was running across the garden with a hosepipe.

More ominously, their ears picked up the barking of dogs. They could see torch beams criss-crossing the lawn like miniature searchlights as dark figures radiated out from the castle to scour the grounds.

'Shall we get out of here?' said Steele. 'I don't think I could bear another of our friend's sanctimonious rants if we were to fall into his clutches again.'

'Me neither,' said Minty. 'He really is a crashing bore.'

'Not to mention that he'll probably torture us to death this time,' said Justin.

12

The three fugitives turned their backs to the house and, moving as fast as they could, headed east towards the outer wall. The ladder was still propped up and waiting where they'd left it earlier. Justin climbed the first few rungs before turning to relieve Minty of the heavy casket. They both glanced anxiously back at Steele, who was watching their movements through glazed eyes, swaying on his feet.

'Are you all right, Daddy?'

'Keep going,' said Steele, slurring his words. 'Don't worry about me. I've been in worse pickles.'

Minty and Justin weren't convinced. Steele sounded drunk, but they knew he'd barely touched a drop of alcohol.

At the top of the wall, Minty reclaimed the casket and began to feel her way down the rungs of a second ladder on the other side. Justin returned to help Steele, whose eyes were now filmy and unfocused. He had a befuddled look and Justin saw to his horror that his future father-in-law's hand was tinged with green. But he swallowed his panic and began methodically to coax the sick man up the ladder. With Justin's help and encouragement, Steele finally reached firm ground on the other side. Waiting next to Minty was a small boy, about ten years old, who was buttoned into a stiff suit with a high collar, though looked as though he would have been more at home in scruffy vest and shorts.

'Jimmy!' said Minty. 'Run ahead and tell your dad to start the car.'

The boy scampered off. Minty and Justin followed more slowly, one on either side of Steele, who was finding it increasingly difficult to walk.

From the direction of the house came the distant cough of straight-eight engines starting up.

'They're coming for us,' said Minty.

When they reached the Rover, semi-concealed in a copse of lime saplings, the engine was already running. Jimmy was holding the door open for them. Minty and Justin half-pushed, half-pulled Steele into the back, and Minty clambered in after him. Justin bundled in after her, and said, 'Step on it, George!' But the driver, dressed in a mechanic's blue overalls, didn't need to be told. Before they'd even got the door closed he was stepping on the accelerator.

The Rover sped through the night. They kept to the back roads, but these were poorly surfaced. Each time they drove over a bump Steele let out a whimper of pain. He slumped further and further sideways until his head was cradled in his daughter's lap. His face was deathly pale, his breath coming in hoarse gasps, but he managed a wry smile.

'Didn't see that one coming! Should have known there'd be a guardian.'

Minty struggled to hold back her tears. 'Don't worry Daddy, we'll get you to a doctor as soon as we reach Prague.'

'Too late!' said Steele. 'The city will be crawling with his minions. We have to go straight to the airfield.'

'But sir...' said Justin.

George piped up from the driver's seat. 'He's right. They'll have road blocks up before you know it, if they're not up already.'

'Oh, Daddy,' said Minty. There was a catch in her voice.

Steele struggled to raise his head. 'Have we got it?'

Justin, clutching the casket, said, 'Got it, sir. It's here! We've got the casket.'

Young Jimmy swivelled in the front seat and planted his chin on the headrest, eyeing the casket with curiosity. His father took a hand off the steering-wheel to prod his arm. 'Sit down, son. Road's going to get even rougher.' Reluctantly, Jimmy obeyed.

Steele's head fell all the way back on to Minty's lap. The greenish tinge was spreading from his arm to his neck and face. 'It's not the casket,' he whispered, so quietly that Minty and Justin had to strain their ears to hear him over the noise of the engine. 'It's what's *inside* that counts.'

'Don't worry Daddy, we'll keep it safe.'

'We should open it,' said Justin. 'It could counter the poison...'

'No!' Steele's voice cracked. 'It's too late. It would only make me more like *him*.'

'There must be *something* we can do,' said Minty.

'He'll come looking for it,' murmured Steele, his voice fading fast. 'They'll all come looking for it...'

'They don't know who we are,' said Justin.

Steele found a last reserve of strength. 'They'll find out. Sooner or later. But promise me you'll never let it fall into their hands...'

'We promise, Daddy.'

'Put a guardian over it...' whispered Steele. There was a faint rasping in his throat, like someone turning a rusty old key in a lock, and then his gaze drifted upwards, through the window, towards the top of the skeletal trees flashing past in the night, towards the full moon.

And the moon gazed back down into his lifeless eyes.

Justin put his arm around Minty's shoulder and held her close as the tears streamed down her face.

CHAPTER 1: GRAPEVINE

The old lady was weeping. She hadn't wept like this since they'd laid her father to rest in the nearby churchyard. But that had been a long, long time ago. Since the distress and regret of that sad occasion, she'd led a very happy life, despite the ever present danger, with her beloved Justin sharing the triumphs and disasters at her side.

They'd travelled and researched and unearthed many rare and valuable artefacts, and foiled a nefarious scheme or two. They'd saved more than a few lives, and although they'd often had to dodge the hunters on their tail, they'd learnt how to protect themselves. They'd loved each other very, very much, and if their union hadn't been blessed with children, well, that was probably for the best, considering the forces that wished them harm.

But that happiness was coming to an end now, because Justin Saxby was on his deathbed. It had been a mercifully swift and relatively painless malady that had felled him, and now it was a dying more natural than they'd ever allowed themselves to hope for, but the occasion was no less sorrowful for that, and it was fraught with anxiety. It had been their bond that had made the glyphs so much stronger, but by the time it dawned on them that the effectiveness had been dependent on their mutual love and regard, it was too late. With one of them gone, the protections they'd meticulously built into Saxby Hall and the land around it wouldn't crumble, but they would be considerably weakened - and at the worst possible time.

'Oh Justy,' she whispered, her tears falling on the the frail old man in the bed. His sight was fading fast, but he managed to squeeze her hand.

'You know what to do when I'm gone.'

'Hush, we've already been through this.'

He made a massive effort to raise his head. 'Defences weakened... Evil forces gathering...'

'They still don't know where it is,' said Minty.

'If I can hold out for just one more week...'

His voice tailed off, the light dimmed from his eyes, and he fell back against the pillow, a sack of skin and bones from which the soul had been expelled.

Minty lowered her head, and sobbed quietly.

There was discreet movement behind her. Frost the factotum had been standing silently in the doorway, watching the scene and wiping away the occasional tear. When he saw it was all over, he turned and left the room, though not through delicacy.

Frost wasn't evil, and he had served the Saxbys long and faithfully, but he was a weak man. His weakness was for money, which he liked to horde rather than spend - ostensibly for his retirement, even though he was already well past the age at which most people stopped working and put their feet up. He had taken regular emoluments from all sides, not seeing the harm in that. The Saxbys had been aware of his duplicity - and indeed Frost himself had been quite open about it - but had never tried to stop him, reasoning that at least this way they knew, more or less, where their enemies were, and what they were up to, and how much they were prepared to pay.

In the library, Frost wiped his eyes on the back of his sleeve, blew his nose noisily on a large cotton handkerchief, and picked up the receiver from its cradle on the ancient Bakelite telephone to make the first of two long distance calls.

*****

It was approaching midnight in Istanbul, and business as usual in the Palace of Pleasure. International oligarchs and high-flying politicians regularly dropped in to cast their scruples aside, along with most of their clothing, leaving them free to frolic out of sight of their puritanical constituencies in a haven where they knew they could indulge in depraved pursuits without fear of admonishment, secure in the knowledge there would always be someone to mop blood off the floor or make witnesses disappear. Some of them paid for this freedom by providing the establishment with sensitive details about arms deals, or treaties, or the off-duty activities of heads of state. The Palace's own archives, stored in the reinforced basement expressly designed to withstand earthquakes of up to a magnitude of 9.0, contained enough compromising material to topple two-thirds of the world's governments, had the management been so inclined. But it was power they wanted, not chaos; in the long term it was more rewarding to maintain a status quo that could be controlled and manipulated than to foment anarchy, amusing though that might have been.

As usual, the air in the main salon was riven by shrieking, but it was hard to tell if the cries were of pleasure or pain. Two giggling houris, clad in silver bikinis, picked their way through a tangle of naked limbs and torsos, stepping carefully over the cats which milled around unchecked, meowing and soliciting scritches. No, it would never do to step on a cat. The taller of the two lovelies was bearing a large gold platter, on which sat a mother-of-pearl telephone. As she and her companion reached the steps leading up to the intended recipient of the phone call, ensconced as usual on the literal throne which provided the perfect vantage point from which to observe the floorshow, the houri with the tray bobbed in a deferential curtsy and announced in Armenian, or possibly some form of Anatolian, 'That call you've been expecting. From England.'

An elegant long-fingered hand, nails lacquered blood red, reached out and beckoned imperiously to the taller houri, who ascended three steps towards the throne and reverentially placed the receiver in the proffered palm. Her petite companion scooped up the end of the cable and plugged it into a socket at the base of the daïs.

*****

Frost's second call went to the Arcadia Hospital in Boston, where it was late afternoon. An administrator picked up the phone, told the caller to hold the line, and made her way through to a scrubbing area where she swiftly slipped into a surgical gown, mask, cap and gloves. In a smartly coordinated movement perfected by long practice, she backed through the swing door into the operating theatre - just as a scalpel sliced cleanly through exposed brain tissue. The Mozart piano sonata tinkling out of hidden speakers was counterpointed by the electronic blip of the monitor recording the patient's heart and respiratory rates. The patient was conscious. The man's eyes were roving from side to side, as if he were trying to see what was happening just out of range of his vision. The atmosphere was one of hushed reverence, as in a church, with the congregation gathered to worship at the altar of the man with the blade.

The administrator slipped past half a dozen robed figures and made straight for the scalpel wielder. To judge from the only part of his face that was visible - watchful grey eyes behind steel-rimmed spectacles - he was a man in his late fifties. The grey eyes flicked momentarily sideways as he sensed the newcomer approaching.

'That call you've been expecting from England, Dr. Ridley,' she murmured, so quietly that only he could hear. 'It came.'

At the word 'England', Ridley promptly lost interest in the exposed cerebellum gleaming in front of him like a delicate strawberry-flavoured blancmange, and handed his scalpel to the nearest robed figure.

'Excuse me, people. I'm afraid you'll have to carry on without me. The fate of humankind hangs in the balance.'

And he followed the administrator out of the theatre, the rest of the surgical staff staring after him in disappointment.

*****

No phone calls were made to a ground-floor flat in Rue des Sorcières, near Montparnasse, but the message got through anyway. The flat was registered as a business, and a small brass plaque by the front entrance attested to its use as an office, but inside, it looked more like a harlot's den, lit by an array of flickering candles and low wattage bulbs glowering beneath red lampshades. The walls were festooned with embroidered shawls, black lace drapes and a series of murky oil paintings depicting a great deal of nakedness and several gruesome killings.

Beneath a small table draped in gauzy saffron-coloured cloth, a man's foot in an Egyptian cotton sock was being caressed by naked, almost prehensile toes, the nails lacquered gold to complement several gold toe-rings. The toes were attached to a shapely foot, which in turn was joined to a well-toned ankle, around which coiled a gleaming gold anklet in the form of a serpent.

Toes, foot and ankle belonged to a dusky-skinned raven-haired beauty with sea-green eyes who was a lot older and wiser than she might have appeared to the lustful eyes of passing men. Her curves sheathed beguilingly in burgundy velvet, she was seated across the table from her latest client, a prosperous-looking fellow in a well-cut business suit who seemed to have difficulty tearing his eyes away from her cleavage, a deep dark trench that promised to swallow him whole, if only he could get near enough.

On the circular table top between them sat a crystal ball, its interior clouded with a swarm of silver pinpricks that eddied and rearranged themselves, like starlings flocking in an ever-changing murmuration. The ball's owner gripped the man's hand as she stared into the swirling cloud, occasionally glancing up to flutter her eyelashes at him.

'I see a voluptuous dark-haired beauty,' she said in slightly accented French, 'and much sexual pleasure ahead...' She smiled seductively, and thought *In your dreams...* Where she was concerned, this phrase wasn't necessarily a figure of speech. In the weeks to come, if all went to plan, the man would be enjoying a series of wet dreams of such seismic intensity they would leave him drained and thoroughly pleasured - with the bedsheets around him sodden, much to his wife's annoyance. And then he would feel compelled to go back to the Rue des Sorcières for another of these 'treatments', which would now cost him twice as much, and not just money...

But it wasn't to be, not this time. The man was almost drooling in fevered anticipation when she spotted something between the silver in the crystal ball: black strands, which invaded the pinpricks like a virus before rearranging themselves into a line of symbols that resembled tiny stick figures kneeling, dancing or tilling the fields. To the casual observer, they might have been Amharic.

Her smile faded, and she gave a weary sigh that seemed to come from the very bottom of her soul, or what was left of it. She had known this day would come; it had been hanging over her for a long time, like a dark cloud on a sunny landscape. Still, a deal was a deal, even if she had been tricked into making it; there was no such thing as cosmic justice, so the best she could hope for was to fulfil her side of the contract so she could once again be left in peace.

She sat up straight in her chair, letting her client's hand flop limply on to the table top, and peered more closely into the crystal ball, her hunched pose oddly reminiscent of a vulture.

Her voice changed. There was a cynical edge to it now.

'Ah, someone has died.'

The man gasped in shock.

'Oh, nothing to do with you, darling.'

She got up, brushed down her skirt, and handed him his shoes and coat.

'But...' he stuttered.

'*Dépêchez-vous!*' she said, clapping her hands. 'I have a date with destiny, *mon ami*, and there's packing to do. A *lot* of packing.'

She ushered him out of the door, murmuring a minor incantation so it wouldn't occur to him to ask for his money back, before returning to the crystal ball to decipher the rest of the message.

'That bastard,' she thought. 'Let's hope this is the last time.'

*****

The next phone call was not from Frost. It went to a powder-blue mobile phone with pink pompoms attached, in a Knightsbridge restaurant teeming with fashion journalists, lesser-known celebrities and a sprinkling of artists whose business sense outshone their actual work. At the sound of the ringtone, configured to imitate the sound of an old-fashioned telephone bell, four airheaded young socialites with preternaturally perfect teeth simultaneously set their Cosmopolitans aside and dove as one into handbags festooned with miniature locks and ostentatious initials that were not their own.

'Not mine!' squealed a brunette.

'Not mine either!' echoed a redhead.

'It's yours, Kitty!' said a smiling blonde.

'Bet it's Hugo,' said the redhead.

A second smiling blonde, with flawless honey-coloured complexion and the prettiest retroussé nose that money could buy, plucked the trilling mobile from her bag while her companions went on chattering about what Blythe had been getting up to with Serena, what Plum had done to Toby, and the extraordinary lengths to which Finn's parents had gone in order to make those pesky accusations disappear.

Kitty Miranda Bridges held the phone up to her ear. A single word was spoken before the caller hung up again. Kitty's smile promptly vanished. It was as though, all of a sudden, she had turned into a completely different person. She hung up, slapped a fifty pound note down on the table, and jumped to her feet.

'Gotta go, girls.'

'Was it Hugo?' asked the redhead.

'Hugo?' Kitty echoed with a puzzled frown, before striding out of the restaurant without a backward glance, leaving her mozzarella and caper salad ungrazed, her Cosmopolitan unsipped, and her companions gawping after her, perplexed.

But only for an instant. The door had barely swung shut behind the departee before the chatter resumed as though it had never been interrupted. But this time with Hugo and his generous trust-fund added to the mix.

*****

Not so very far away geographically, but culturally on an entirely different planet, another scene was playing out in Goldhawk Road, in west London. Dark Star

Recording Studios was throbbing to the heavy beat of rock music loud enough to make the average eardrum bleed. Every so often the commotion was intensified by a shrieking wall of solid feedback or a blast of deafening white noise. Luckily for the drummer, singer and keyboard player, they felt no pain, for their hearing had already been shredded by exposure to many years of this cacophony.

Of the quartet, only the lean, mean bass player retained perfect hearing, thanks to the glyphs traced on his tympanic membranes with a gold needle dipped in jellyfish venom, and he had long since perfected the technique of hearing only what he chose to listen to. He was dressed in black leather trousers so form-fitting they resembled ballet tights, and a strategically ripped T-shirt emblazoned with a collage of obscenities and Tom of Finland artwork.

The long-haired sound engineer, who was dropping ash over the mixing desk in the control room, jammed his fist down on the intercom button.

'That was really cool guys. Let's do it again.'

'One two three,' said the singer, and the band members launched into a horrible caterwauling chord which ebbed and flowed for nearly a minute before the technician interrupted.

'Griff, man. Someone to see you. Says it can't wait.'

The bass player looked over at the glass-fronted control booth and saw a sultry brunette beckoning to him with her long gold-painted fingernails.

His cadaverous face, its allure oddly enhanced by a sprinkling of pockmarks and carelessly applied eyeliner, erupted into a toothy grin.

'Noreen! *Mon amour!*'

The bass player (whose birth name had been Daystar, which he'd changed to Derek before finally settling on Griff) unplugged his guitar and strode towards the door.

*****

Meanwhile, in a drab North London suburb, a pallid nerd sat cross-legged like a tailor on the floor of his cluttered first-floor flat over a shop selling second-hand furniture that nobody ever wanted to buy, not least because the place was nearly always closed. He was sitting in a small clearing amid heaps of yellowing newsprint, half-eaten takeaways, and toppling stacks of crumbling books and pre-digital files. It was fortunate he was a non-smoker, because his surroundings were the very definition of fire risk; a single spark, and the room would have gone up like a bonfire. The nerd's spectacles reflected fragments of the images flickering across the screen of a nearby television with the sound off. Early Pink Floyd droned gently from a tape deck in the corner of the room.

Brian Orville Curtis was busy snipping out a magazine article titled *The New Wave of Hipster Occultists* when his attention was caught by a photograph of a distinguished-looking man which flashed up on the TV screen. He immediately dropped the scissors and picked up the remote control, turning up the volume so he could hear it over *A Saucerful of Secrets.*

'... the death of Justin Saxby, the archaeologist and antiquary best known for his discovery of the Rift Valley codex, and his pivotal role in exposing the

Strickland-Dwyer neo-Nazi spy ring. A spokesman from the Royal Archaeological Institute paid tribute today in a...'

Curtis took a long sip from his mug of weak tea (the third he'd managed to squeeze out of one teabag), still staring at the images flickering across the television screen. When the news switched to another item he turned the volume down again and, humming along to *Set the Controls for the Heart of the Sun*, reached for a buff-coloured file marked CASTLE PRETORIUS.

*****

Its scales etched in blue and green, the snake stretched all the way around the waist and ended, Ouroboros-style, with its tail in its own maw, representing the infinite cycle of life itself, though it was safe to say its wearer had never given a second's though to the symbolism of his tattoo. Least of all while he was so intent on giving the woman beneath him a solid South London in-and-out.

Victor Ignatius Pearce's naked buttocks moved up and down to a primitive caveman rhythm audible only to himself, and certainly not to Diane, who had reached her climax five minutes earlier. Her attention had already started to wander; right now she was thinking about the best day to get her roots retouched.

The buttocks themselves were still admirably taut. The rest of Vic's physique landed somewhere between rangy and wiry, though a lifelong beer habit, instigated by a sneaky sip of IPA at the age of seven, was now starting to show around his midriff. He'd already made a resolution to spend more time at the gym, though it was unlikely he'd ever act on it, given that power squats and abdominal crunches bored him silly.

Still, he was getting a work-out now. After a great deal of energetic pumping, Vic finally shot his wad with a strangled cry and flopped sideways.

'You remind me of my old man,' sighed Diane, at long last able to light the fag for which she'd been gagging for the last five minutes. She wasn't a bad looking bird, but she wore far too much make-up, even in bed. Some of it had come off on the pillow.

'Wish I had your old man's money,' said Vic, reaching over to nick one of her cigarettes.

'If you had his money I'd be married to *you*,' said Diane. She ran her free hand over his abdomen. 'Do you think I should get a tattoo? Where'd you get this anyway?'

'China,' said Vic. 'All the gangsters have them there.'

'You're having me on. You've never been to China.'

'Got me there, Diane. Actually was Margate. Your old man's stag party, in fact. Bit of a lost weekend, that. Don't remember much about it, to be honest. Just woke up on the Monday, and bingo! There it was.'

Not for the first time, he squinted down at the blue and green scales in bewilderment. A tattoo that big and intricate, he calculated, would have taken days to complete, multiple visits to the tattooist, and a shitload of pain. Yet it had appeared on him virtually overnight... and he didn't remember a thing.

Diane sighed. 'Oh gawd, not Margate again. He never stops bragging about that bloody weekend.'

'It was legendary. Or so I'm told.'

'Did they ever find the missing stripper?'

Vic frowned. All he knew was that there were some memories it was better not to recover. 'I don't know, love. But your old man had the time of his life, and that's all that matters.'

Diane pouted. 'How could he have the time of his life when I wasn't even there? Had the time of his life afterwards, on his *honeymoon*, you mean.'

'Yeah, of course,' said Vic.

'Well, your snake is dead sexy.'

Her hand strayed further down, but before it could reach the South Pole, the bedroom door burst open and two goons sauntered in, casual as you like, as if they owned the place. Vic sat up straight and tried to look insouciant, like a choirboy caught playing with himself. Diane huddled down in the bed, pulling the sheet up over her face.

'Hello, Pearce,' said the bigger of the goons, whose neck was almost as wide as his head.

'Fuck off, Jeff. Can't you see I've got company?'

'Mr. Turlingham wants a word,' said the thin goon, whose scarred face was so gaunt it could have passed for a death's head in the dim light filtering through the curtains.

'Later,' said Vic.

'*Now,*' said Fat Jeff. 'Or do you need persuading?' He curled his fingers into a fist, the wistful expression on his fleshy face hinting that he hoped Vic would say 'yes'.

Vic could be dumb, and frequently was, but he wasn't *that* dumb. Cursing, he rolled out of bed and pulled on his trousers. He didn't normally go commando but under the circumstances, he reasoned, the Y-Fronts could wait. Before he'd even got the flies zipped, Fat Jeff gripped his arm and started yanking him towards the door. Vic managed to grab his T-shirt and jacket on the way there. The thin goon picked up Vic's shoes and turned back to the bed.

'Want a lift, ma'am?'

Diane peeked over the top of the sheet. 'Thanks, Tony, but no. I'll get there under my own steam.'

'OK then,' said Thin Tony. 'See you later, Mrs. Turlingham.'

*****

The surface of the antique oriental desk was cluttered with an incongruous combination of ancient artefacts and modern executive toys. Pudgy fingers, around one of them a chunky gold ring embellished with an ancient circular symbol, drummed impatiently on the lacquered wood. The pudgy fingers were attached to a pudgy hand, and the hand belonged, like the desk, to the man sitting behind it. Everything in the room belonged to him, including the people now gathered there.

'Associate of mine just passed away,' said Turlingham in a gravel-throated London accent which betrayed a lifelong addiction to torpedo-sized cigars, one of which he was puffing away at now, in between snacking from the bowl of stuffed olives or quaffing from the man-sized glass of red wine in front of him.

Jimmy Turlingham was the sort of barrel-chested bruiser who even in his seventies could probably have gone ten rounds with Henry Cooper in his prime, but his employees still called him 'Little Jimmy' behind his back. To his face they called him 'Guv' or 'Boss', but he preferred to be addressed as 'Sir', or, even better, 'Sir James'. Somewhere at the back of his brain he still harboured fantasies of a knighthood, but despite generous contributions to South London charities, and framed photographs showing him cosying up to the likes of Bobby Moore, Geoff Hurst and Princess Margaret, this was an ambition never to be realised, thanks to a long and very public history of extortion, racketeering and sexual deviance.

Behind him stood Thin Tony, cleaning his fingernails with a cut-throat razor.

'Bit of a toff, he was,' said Turlingham. He stopped drumming to set in motion a Newton's Cradle. The silver balls click-clacked. 'Never knew Mr. Saxby, did you Vic?'

Vic, now fully dressed but rumpled, was perched uncomfortably on the smooth edge of a cream-coloured leather sofa. It took considerable effort not to slither off.

'Never had that pleasure,' he said.

Turlingham placed his hand on the ornate gold casket taking pride of place among the artefacts. 'He was a gentleman, but a thief. Nicked this, he did. Lovely piece. Worth a lot of money, he said. Then he sold it to me, as was his wont.'

The door opened. Diane slipped into the room, her attempts at being inconspicuous stymied at the first hurdle by the shimmering sequinned gown clinging to her curves. Vic's was the only head that didn't turn to stare.

'Hello love,' said Turlingham. 'Glad you could join us. Make yourself comfortable.'

Diane looked anything but comfortable as she took the only free seat in the room, which happened to be on the sofa next to Vic. She sat down as far from him as possible, crossed her long legs with an evocative swish of nylon, and began to chain-smoke sulkily.

Turlingham continued. 'But do you know, Vic? Mr. Saxby was having a laugh at my expense. Because only later did I find out that the box itself is worthless. It was the contents that was worth all that money. The contents. And he kept them for himself, like the gentleman he was.'

Vic's curiosity was aroused. 'So what was the contents?'

Turlingham smiled, without warmth or humour. 'That's what I want you to find out. Take a little trip to Norfolk. You do know where Norfolk is, don't you Vic?'

Vic repeated a remark he had once heard. 'Very flat, Norfolk.' The beginnings of a smirk were wiped off his face when he saw Turlingham's expression.

'Have a word with the widow Saxby. And have it quick, because I hear I'm not the only interested party. You might have to... *persuade* her to part with whatever it is, know what I mean?'

'Yeah, right,' said Vic.

Turlingham flicked a stuffed olive high into the air. Quick as a flash, Thin Tony dipped forward to slice it in half with his razor, exposing the red innards. The two halves of the olive fell to the floor.

'Because if you come back without it, there *will* be consequences, know what I mean?'

Vic knew. He swallowed noisily.

Luckily for him, the sound of his gulp was drowned out by the click-clack of the silver balls.

CHAPTER 2: THE FUNERAL

Vic's mustard-coloured Z-registration Opel Manta had seen better days, but despite the occasional tubercular splutter from the engine, it did its job efficiently enough as it bore its driver from the inner city streets of Lewisham, through leafy suburbs and on to the northbound motorway.

Eventually, even the motorway gave up, consigning the car to narrow roads skirting towns, passing through deserted villages and needlessly twisting their way through an increasingly desolate landscape. The countryside was flat and open to the elements, criss-crossed by the occasional muddy brown canal.

The roads grew so narrow that, had he met another vehicle, he would have been obliged to pull over on to the unkempt verge to let it pass. But there were no other vehicles. The only point of interest was the distant horizon, and Vic kept his eyes fixed on it, trying manfully not to doze off at the wheel. Every so often, at a junction, he would pause to consult his dog-eared map, but the further he drove, the more that chart seemed like a work of fiction, the markings bearing scant relation to the roads laid out in front of him. His cursing became more frequent. This was the back of beyond. He was a city boy, a long way out of his comfort zone.

The wintery sun was low in the sky when he reached the stream. According to the map, there wasn't even supposed to be a bridge there, but by now Vic was used to its omissions, additions and all-round creative approach to topography. Like the Opel lurching over it, the bridge had seen better days. Whatever the local council was, Vic reflected, they clearly didn't pay much attention to the upkeep of this corner of their bailiwick. But he wasn't too worried; the water was shallow, and the drop no more than a couple of feet, for which he was thankful. He'd had a problem with heights ever since being dangled off the side of Blackfriars Bridge by a pair of vengeful bootleggers.

From here on, the route seemed more straightforward. After twenty minutes of uncertainty, he reached a signpost pointing to Saxby Hall, which reassured him that he was heading in the right direction. Not long after that, he spotted a stunted Norman church surrounded by an overgrown graveyard. Graveyards always gave him the willies, so he was about to accelerate past when he spotted the parking area near the gates. It was already jammed with cars, including, he noted covetously, a shiny red Alfa Romeo convertible. Up ahead, nearer the church, he spied a knot of dark figures.

A funeral was in progress.

How many funerals could there possibly be in this neck of the woods, today of all days? Vic's spirits lifted. He'd arrived just as they were laying Justin Saxby to rest. Maybe the fates were smiling on him after all, and he wouldn't even need to travel as far as Saxby Hall. Maybe he could sort out this business right now and head back home before nightfall.

He stopped the car, got out, and lit a cigarette. The winding path seemed to be taking him away from the knot of figures, not towards it, so he boldly plunged off the path and started to pick his way through the overgrowth. As he waded through the long grass he noticed a tall man, shoulders slightly hunched, clutching a bunch of drooping white chrysanthemums in front of a moss-covered headstone. The man looked furtively around to check he wasn't being observed, drew a small flask out of his pocket, and raised it to his lips. As Vic drew level, their eyes met for an instant. The tall man hurriedly pocketed the flask and pretended to be laying the chrysanthemums on the grave in front of him before piously clasping his hands in prayer. But by the time Vic looked back, a few paces further on, he had already abandoned the charade and got his flask out again.

But this was no more than a sideshow to the main action up ahead. A couple of dozen sombrely dressed figures were clustered around a gleaming white coffin by the side of a freshly dug grave. Judging by the configuration of the small crowd, the service had yet to begin, but standing in pole position at the graveside, next to a monument engraved with the name Quentin 'Tiger' Steele ('Headed Forth to Explore the Great Unknown') was a diminutive female figure draped in a black veil. She was conversing intently with the vicar. Probably letting him know what she wanted him to say about her dearly departed, Vic surmised.

Well, let's get this over with, he thought and sidled towards the gathering.

Heads turned as he shambled past, cigarette dangling from his lips.

'Mrs. Saxby?'

The woman wheeled round to face him, gasped and reeled back in distress, almost as though his hardman reputation had preceded him, though Vic was confident she couldn't possibly know him from Adam. He was about to address her again when he felt bony fingers clamping his arm. He shook himself free, and turned to see a gaunt man in a shabby black suit.

'Sir. This isn't the time or the place.'

'Turlingham sent me,' said Vic.

'I don't care if Mahatma Gandhi sent you,' said the man. 'It can wait. Have you no respect?'

The man looked to be in his sixties, at least. Had he been the only one present, Vic could have dealt with him easily, but some of the other mourners were also glaring in his direction. None of them looked particularly tough, but Vic sensed that instigating a brawl at the graveside wouldn't help his cause. Reluctantly, he withdrew about fifty feet and stationed himself beneath a large yew to light another cigarette.

As the coffin was lowered into the grave and the widow leant forward to cast a handful of earth in after it, Vic's eye was caught by movement among the graves to his right. A couple had broken away from the main gathering and set up their own little ceremony out of sight of the other mourners. Vic did a double-take. The man was wearing black leather trousers which had been peeled down around his knees, exposing pasty buttocks. Kneeling in front of him was a woman with skin the colour of cinnamon, whose low-cut black velvet dress exposed an eye-popping amount of cleavage as she swayed rhythmically to and fro. Vic felt his own trousers fill out as he realised what the woman was doing with her mouth. At a funeral, yet! She seemed to be concentrating too hard on the task at hand to notice anything else, but even as he stared in astonishment she raised a gloved hand and waved gaily to him.

Vic quickly looked away, simultaneously aroused and embarrassed.

*****

The mourners began to disperse, crossing the graveyard in dribs and drabs to where their cars were parked. Vic returned to his Opel and, as the first group drove off, followed at a prudent distance.

It was just as well they were leading the way. After several tangents along dirt roads, he doubted he could ever have located the destination on his own. But maybe these were short cuts, because only ten minutes later he found himself driving past a stone pillar with the words 'Saxby Hall' carved into it. The wrought iron gates were open. He drove through them, up a long winding drive to a gravel terrace in front of a compact 18th Century mansion, its relative modesty compromised by an incongruously grand portico.

Vic parked between a Range Rover and a Mercedes. Further along, next to a black cab, was the red Alfa Romeo he'd already spotted at the graveyard. Evidently the late Mr. Saxby's associates weren't short of cash. Vic got out of his car and walked the rest of the way and up the steps leading to the entrance. The door was standing open, but that was as far as he got. The gaunt man in the shabby black suit cordially but firmly barred his way.

'You'll have to come back tomorrow, sir. Mrs. Saxby is in no state to talk business.'

'I've come all the way from London,' said Vic.

'Nothing to be proud of, sir. Some of these people have crossed oceans to be here.'

Vic peered past the man's shoulder into a vast wainscotted hall where a dozen or so mourners were already clustered together in a small knot, sipping glasses of sherry and making small talk. They seemed uneasy; Vic noticed some of them glancing uncomfortably at the parquet, as though they yearned to wander off and explore the rest of the house, but there was something unseen that prevented them from doing so. The hall was surprisingly ill-kempt; someone had spilled salad in one of the doorways leading off it, and at the bottom of the staircase the floor was sprinkled with what appeared to be chalk dust, or possibly salt. Mrs. Saxby really needed to sack her cleaning staff and find more efficient replacements, Vic thought. Then again, maybe the servants were as old as she was, and sentimentality had encouraged her to overlook their sloppiness. You never knew with the upper classes. The ones he'd had dealings with in the past had all had money problems, and they'd all been mad as hatters.

'Who the fuck are you anyway?' Vic asked the man in the shabby suit. 'Her bodyguard?'

The man inclined his head. 'Frost, sir. The factotum.'

'Pleased to meet you, Frosty the factotum,' said Vic. He put his hand on the man's shoulder and prepared to shove him aside. But he could feel unexpectedly taut sinew beneath his fingers, and Frost gave him such a withering glare he removed them, feeling slightly embarrassed.

'Tomorrow, sir,' said Frost. His voice had acquired a menacing edge.

Vic looked around at the featureless countryside in despair. 'And where am I supposed to stay in the meantime?'

Frost made a grating noise in his throat that might conceivably have been laughter.

'Only one place in these parts, sir.'
He issued Vic with directions.

*****

Vic had been driving along the coast road for so long it felt as though he'd left England behind and had broken through into an offshore netherworld swept by salty waves and navigated by scruffy seabirds which wheeled and screeched into the stinging wind. The tide was a long way out, leaving endless mudflats as far as the eye could see, punctuated by a few gnarled and stunted growths only an incurable optimist would have described as trees.

At last, at the end of a single-track road, his destination hove into view. The sight made him want to turn around and drive straight back the way he'd come.

'You have got be fucking kidding,' he said out loud.

The inn squatted on the horizon like a hunchback, its warped gables and chimneys forming a grim blot on an already grim landscape, made even grimmer by the gathering dusk, which was rapidly leaching the scene of all hues other than drab variations on black and ashen. Even then, the black didn't look like a *real* black; it was more an absence - of light, warmth and anything resembling life.

As Vic drew nearer, his eyes made out a timbered gibbet with a pub sign hanging from it. On the sign were the establishment's name and a crude painting of the upper half of a man. Whatever had removed the absent lower half, it had been a clean cut, with only a daub of red and mauve around the untethered waist to indicate the separation had not been a gentle one.

The Half Man wasn't listed in the Great British Bread & Breakfast Guide, that was for sure.

Vic parked out in front next to a Morris Minor Traveller even more antiquated than his Opel, took his bag out of the boot, and reluctantly approached the front door.

Inside, the inn was no more welcoming than its exterior, but at least it was warmer, thanks to a pile of glowing logs in the open fireplace. The only sounds were the ticking of a grandfather clock which was showing a time of day that bore scant relation to the one indicated by Vic's wristwatch, and a soft scurrying from the walls which might have been mice, or cockroaches.

It was The Pub That Time Forgot. In pride of place next to the door was a framed certificate testifying to a Silver Saucepan Award from the North Norfolk Guide to Pub Nosh, a publication that had gone out of business a couple of decades earlier according to a handwritten caption beneath Festival of Britain-era graphics. The stone walls were hung with faded photographs, rusty mantraps, and antediluvian firearms that looked as though any attempt to fire them would backfire horribly on the shooter. In an apparent concession to the Twentieth Century, there was also a range of entertainment: bar billiards, dartboard, upright piano, and a chunky jukebox dating from, at a guess, the sixties.

Vic's spirits plunged, then picked up again when he saw the bar was fully stocked. After his epic journey, he was in dire need of a drink.

'Hello?'

No reply. Nothing except the faint ticking and scurrying. To the left of the bar was an open doorway. He stuck his head through it, and was met by a faceful of cold air. Worn stone steps led down into darkness; evidently some sort of cellar.

'Can I help you?'

Vic jumped guiltily, as though he'd been caught with his hand in the till. He turned to find a tall, thin woman who might have been in her forties. The dark hair flecked with grey was scraped back into a strict bun, and her calf-length charcoal-grey dress was shapeless and drab, but she was well-preserved and not unattractive; it was as though she were deliberately trying to appear as unalluring as possible. Tied loosely around her waist was an apron smeared with red and purple, as though she'd been bottling jam. She stepped in front of Vic, firmly closed the cellar door and turned back to fix him with a searching gaze.

'I'd like a room,' said Vic.

The woman shook her head. 'We're full.'

Vic couldn't believe his ears. 'Full? How can you be full? This is the middle of nowhere!'

'Busiest night in years, sir. The Saxby funeral.'

'Just been there,' said Vic. 'Got business with the widow in the morning.'

The woman gave Vic another searching look, as though trying to scan his thoughts. He squirmed uncomfortably, like a naughty schoolboy confronted by a stern headmistress. At length she said, 'In that case, I'll see what we can do.'

She rummaged beneath the bar before handing Vic a large, old-fashioned key. 'Not fancy, but better than nothing. Up the stairs, first on the left. I'll make up the bed for you later. Bathroom and toilet on the right.'

'Thanks, Mrs... er..'

'Mrs. Rock,' she said.

Vic took the key, which weighed as much as a small safe, and made his way up the stairs. Each tread groaned beneath his weight, but he managed to reach the landing without any of them giving way. A single lightbulb burned from the ceiling of a gloomy passageway lined with doors. At the far end, a modern picture window looked out across the windswept marshland. Vic couldn't think why anyone might want to install a window there to frame such a dismal view.

A sudden draught made him shiver. Quickly, he inserted his key into the lock on the first door on the left. It opened on to a small, shabby room with a sloping floor and a low ceiling criss-crossed with oppressive beams. A couple of faded watercolour landscapes hung on either side of a mirror so old most of the silvering had worn off. The bed was narrow and, when he tested it, excessively soft and lumpy.

Vic dumped his bag and went over to the window. The view wasn't quite identical to the one from the landing window, but it might as well have been. Beyond his Opel and the Morris Minor lay the same endless flat and windswept marshland. Dusk was giving way to night. His attention was caught by a small light in the distance, a will o' the wisp quivering a few feet over the ground. Only very gradually did it dawn on him that the light was a bicycle lamp. He stared at it, mesmerised, as it jiggled and bobbed, slowly coming nearer.

The impact of a door slamming downstairs made the room shake, and wrenched him out of his daze.

Jesus Christ almighty, he thought, shaking his head. *So this is what they do for entertainment around here.*

He turned back towards the stairs.

*****

The fire had been stoked and the logs were crackling merrily. Mrs. Rock had disappeared, but taking her place behind the bar was a tall man wiping glasses with a grimy teatowel in between taking sips from a generous tumbler of whisky. His face looked vaguely familiar, but it wasn't until Vic had requested and received a pint of Black Monk that he remembered where he'd seen the bloke before: tippling from a hip flask in the graveyard.

The fellow looked so miserable that Vic thought it politic not to mention their earlier encounter. He drank beer in silence for a while before getting out a cigarette. 'Got an ashtray?'

The barman crossed to Vic's table and placed a battered tin ashtray in front of him.

'Funerals,' he sighed. 'Not my idea of fun.'

'Nor mine,' said Vic, relieved to have found someone he could commiserate with. 'Name's Vic, by the way.'

'Zachary Rock,' said the man, holding out his hand. Vic shook it. Despite his drinking habit, Rock's grip was as solid as his name.

'Another of those?' he asked.

Vic drained his almost empty glass and nodded.

'I was told this place was full,' he said as Rock returned to his position behind the bar and started to draw another pint. 'Doesn't look full to me.'

'Give it time,' said Rock.

As if on cue, there was an ear-shattering crash as the door to the inn was flung open.

Vic looked up, expecting to see a bruiser as big as the sound. But standing in the doorway was a weedy figure with the sort of face that, had it belonged to a schoolboy, would have been just begging to be bullied. His crumpled navy blue suit was partly covered by a shabby green anorak, of the sort habitually worn by birdwatchers. His trouser legs were cinched in with bicycle clips.

The new arrival shuffled up to the bar. 'Shandy, if you please, my good man.'

Rock looked exasperated. He finished drawing Vic's second pint before pouring out the shandy.

The newcomer picked up both drinks and brought them over to Vic. 'I believe this is yours,' he said, placing the Black Monk on the table.

Vic nodded offhandedly and took a sip of his beer.

'Bit nippy for this time of year,' said the man in the anorak.

Vic ignored him. Undaunted, the man stuck out his hand.

'Brian Curtis, not of this parish.'

Vic opened his mouth to tell him to fuck off. He wasn't here to make small talk. But before he could form the words, there was a roar and a ruckus of engines outside. The window was lit up by headlights, followed by the sound of car doors slamming in relay.

Brian Curtis took a gulp of shandy and laughed shakily.

'Here they come,' he said.

CHAPTER 3: CRANIAL GLAIVE

Vic lit another cigarette, but Curtis just leant closer, whispering into his ear, 'The man in leather trousers. Keep your eye on him. He's the one.'

Vic tried to hide his discomfort. Was this puny specimen making a pass at him? He pretended he hadn't heard, but the words 'leather trousers' made him think back to the couple at the graveyard. The idea that this godforsaken hinterland might somehow be teeming with swingers both dismayed and excited him.

Curtis gulped down the rest of his shandy and went back to the bar. 'Same again, my good man,' he said, pushing his empty glass towards Rock, who glared at it with ill-concealed contempt.

But Vic was more interested in the vision that had suddenly appeared in the doorway. Poised there, like a celebrated actress preparing to make her grand entrance on to a provincial stage, was the woman in black velvet. He would have recognised her instantly even if she hadn't raised a gloved hand to wave at him again, but now his view of her was unimpeded by buttocks, he could see she was spectacular.

She strolled into the bar, followed by two men. The skinny punk in leather trousers was almost certainly the owner of the naked backside in the graveyard. There was more metal embedded in this bloke's ears, nose and eyebrows than one might find in the average cutlery drawer. On his T-shirt, strategically ripped to reveal one of the nipple-piercings underneath, was a drawing of a Nazi sodomising a man in a cowboy hat.

The second man couldn't have presented more of a contrast. He was robust but trim, his suit the model of moneyed discretion. He looked older, possibly in his fifties, with distinguished silver hair, platinum-rimmed spectacles and an air of natural authority that made him appear taller than he actually was. As he stepped over the threshold he paused, allowing his grey eyes to sweep the room and register the presence of Vic, Brian Curtis and Mr. Rock. The glance was fleeting as the beam from a lighthouse, but Vic had the uncomfortable impression it had been enough for the silver-haired newcomer to ascertain everything there was to know about him.

The man's expression was benign, though, as he resumed his journey to the bar, where Rock acknowledged him with a curt but deferential nod. 'Dr. Ridley. What can I get you?'

'The usual, please, Mr. Rock. And for my associates...' He glanced over his shoulder. 'Tequila on the rocks and a pint of bitter.'

Curtis had retreated with his shandy to the bench by the window. He was sitting up like a meerkat, staring petrified at the leather-trousered punk as he sauntered over to the jukebox and browsed the tracks on offer.

'Bloody hell, haven't you got anything later than 76?' The punk pressed a couple of coins into the slot and almost immediately began to pogo madly to a deafening blast of T. Rex's *Get It On*.

At the bar, Ridley winced. 'For Christ's sake, Griff. We've just come from a funeral. Turn that racket down.' He didn't need to raise his voice to make himself heard over the music, but Griff ignored him and carried on pogoing, leaving Rock to scurry over to the jukebox and lower the volume.

Vic, meanwhile, was finding it hard to tear his gaze away from the woman in black velvet. Diane had a nice figure, he thought, but this bird was something else. All of a sudden, the prospect of spending the night in this dump didn't seem quite so dreary.

The woman sensed him staring, returned his gaze without a trace of coyness, and sashayed towards him, unlit cigarette dangling from her lips, seemingly held in place by nothing more than her scarlet lipstick.

'Got a light, big boy?'

'Name's Vic,' he said, grabbing his Bic to light her cigarette. 'Vic Pearce.'

'Vic Pearce,' she repeated, blowing smoke from her nostrils. 'You can call me Noreen, if you like. Noreen Duval.'

'You staying here too?'

'Only place in town.' She winked, and Vic felt a thrill in his loins.

Noreen's leather-trousered companion stopped pogoing and sidled up to join them. 'Watch out, mate. She'll have you for breakfast.'

'I'm always up for the full English,' said Vic.

Noreen chuckled, and Vic felt his trousers tighten around his groin. She was laughing at his joke! Always a good sign.

'Rules me out,' she said. 'Irish dam, French sire.'

'But I like Continental too,' Vic added quickly.

Griff snorted. 'Don't forget couscous. She's a right little mongrel, this one. And she bites. I'd be careful if I were you, mate.'

A sudden 'Ha!' made Vic turn his head. Over by the window, Curtis's eyes were bulging out of their sockets. Vic wondered if the little bloke was on drugs, though he didn't seem the druggy type. Unlike this leather-trousered punk, whose constant fidgeting implied he'd already been imbibing something stronger than caffeine.

Curtis saw Vic looking back at him, jerked his head towards Griff and mouthed the word, *HIM*. He drained his shandy and crossed back to the bar to plonk down the empty glass.

'Give me a double scotch, my good man.'

This time, Rock couldn't keep the sneer off his face. 'I'm not your *good man*.'

Curtis looked hurt. 'Just trying to be chummy.'

Vic switched his attention back to Griff, who was now ambling around the bar, fiddling with the ancient weaponry on the walls. He poked a finger into the barrel of a primitive pistol and wiggled it lasciviously, making a face like an actor in a Carry On film. He tickled a rusty halberd, and ran his hand over a spiked mace, mouthing another exaggerated 'oooh!' as one of the spikes scored a deep scratch into his palm. Slowly and deliberately, he licked the blood seeping from the laceration.

Vic's rising disgust was nipped in the bud as Noreen sat down next to him. She crossed her legs, and from the corner of his eye he caught a glint of something shiny. He looked down. Coiled around her ankle was a gold snake, tail clasped in its own mouth.

It wasn't a real snake, of course, but an anklet. For a moment he fancied it was moving, but no, it was just the firelight glancing off the gold.

Tail clasped in its own mouth.

Just like his tattoo, in fact. For a moment, lulled by the shimmer of the anklet, Vic felt on the verge of grasping something significant... But the spell was shattered by a hoarse screech.

He looked up in alarm. Griff had wrapped his hands around the hilt of a sword and was drawing it slowly out of a rusty sheath which was protesting with a high-pitched metallic shriek that set everyone's teeth on edge; worse than fingernails on a chalkboard. When the sword was finally liberated from its casing, the punk launched into a series of flamboyant samurai poses that hinted at much practising in front of a mirror.

Vic shifted uneasily as the blade whizzed through the air only a few inches from his shoulder.

'Oi, watch it,' he growled.

Rock looked over from where he was wiping glasses with a filthy teatowel. 'Put that back, sir. It's worth a lot of money.'

Curtis, looking from Griff to Rock and back again to Griff, piped up. 'It is, in fact, a particularly well-crafted replica of a twelfth century cranial glaive.'

'Griff!' Ridley spoke without even looking up from his lager. 'Put it down.'

As though it were entirely his own decision and nothing to do with Ridley's command, Griff lost interest in the sword, dropping it with a clatter on top of the jukebox. Meanwhile, to Vic's disappointment, Noreen stood up and deserted him for Curtis, who squirmed in discomfort as she approached.

'And where are you from, little man? I didn't see you at the funeral.'

Griff sniggered. 'Can't see much from a kneeling position, darling.'

It was obvious to Vic that Curtis was terrified. The little man made several abortive attempts to speak before finally coming out with, 'I currently reside in the vicinity of New Barnet but I...'

He broke off as Noreen leant forward to blow a cloud of smoke into his face. Then finished his speech with a rush. 'But I was actually born in Paddington. Not that I'm a trainspotter or anything.'

Ridley looked up from his beer, suddenly interested. 'So what *do* you spot, Mr.... Curtis, isn't it? What exactly was your connection to the late Justin Saxby?'

'Yes, do tell,' said Noreen. She slowly began to peel off her gloves, revealing long and elegant fingers tipped by golden nail varnish.

Curtis seemed emboldened by the attention. He tapped the side of his nose in a theatrical gesture. 'That's for me to know and you to find out.'

Ridley frowned and seemed about to question him further, but his train of thought was interrupted by the sound of another vehicle drawing up outside, the heavy chugging of its engine accompanied by a fresh set of headlights sweeping the room through the window.

Everyone turned to blink at the light except Noreen and Vic, who watched disbelievingly as she began to extract items from her handbag: rectangular make-up mirror, small plastic sachet, razor blade. She tipped a sizeable quantity of white powder from the sachet on to the mirror and, making no attempt to conceal her actions, began to chop at it with the blade.

Vic was impressed by her brazenness, but Rock grimaced. 'I'd rather you didn't do that, madam.'

'Oh, who gives a flying fuck,' said Griff, and grinned around the room at nobody in particular. 'What are we waiting for? Might as well get this party started.'

Headlights swept the room again, casting a momentary spotlight over his skinny figure as the vehicle moved off. In one fluid movement, Griff drained his beer glass and smashed it against a nearby chair. Then picked up the largest glass shard and, as though it were the most natural thing in the world, began to carve a symbol into the flesh of his forearm. Blood welled up and began to trickle down the arm.

Vic looked on aghast. Was this bloke a maniac or what? He couldn't be doing with these hippie types. Or punks, or whatever they were. Their values were not like his. They had no respect for tradition. You couldn't even threaten them with violence, because they were already into creative self-harm. He looked over at Ridley and Noreen, neither of whom was showing the slightest discombobulation at their associate's behaviour. Business as usual, apparently.

But Curtis was nodding slowly and meaningfully, as if to say *I told you so.*

Rock resignedly dragged a broom across the floor and began to corral the broken glass into a neat pile. Vic watched approvingly. Here, at least, was a geezer who knew his place in the pecking order. Maybe Mrs. Saxby should hire him to sweep the salad off her floor. As he stared semi-hypnotised at the brisk movements of the broom, he became aware of a dainty pair of feet tripping across the floor. Strappy pink sandals, with high heels. Not practical wear for this terrain, nor for the time of year. Vic watched the sandals for a bit before his gaze strayed up, taking in the bare, lightly tanned legs before continuing past a trim pink designer suit to a flawless face framed in impeccably coiffed blonde hair.

The young woman was dressed as if for summer lunch at Harvey Nichols. From one of her arms hung a big leather tote bag; her other hand brandished a powder-blue mobile phone garnished with sparkly pink pom-poms. She glanced at Griff's bloody handiwork and, automatically assuming she had everyone's undivided attention, addressed the room. 'Yuck, that's so gross. Could somebody bring my bags in? Do you know, I just can't get a signal.'

Rock paused in his sweeping. 'You can forget about using that thing around here, love. This is one big dead spot. You'll just have to use the land line, like everyone else.'

The blonde rolled her big blue eyes in exasperation. 'You'll be telling me next you don't have an internet connection.'

Noreen looked up from where she was arranging white powder into neat lines, smiled and said, 'Miaow.'

Ridley stepped forward. 'May I offer you a drink, Miss... Bridges, isn't it?'

'Why thank you, Dr. Ridley,' said the blonde. 'You can call me Kitty. I'll have a glass of champagne.'

Rock produced a bottle of Asti Spumante and filled a sherry glass. Kitty took one sip and wrinkled her nose. 'What *is* this?'

Ridley was staring at her with unabashed curiosity. 'I hope you don't mind me asking, Kitty, but how did you get here? Did someone give you a ride?'

53

Kitty shrugged. 'Taxi. What else?'

'Really?' said Ridley. 'Quite a distance from the nearest station, I would have thought.'

Kitty stared back at him as though he'd said something stupid. 'What station? I caught it right in front of Harrods.'

'Ah yes, of course.' Ridley's mouth twitched, as though he was trying to keep a straight face. 'I'll just... nip outside and bring in those bags for you.'

Unlike Ridley, Vic was openly nonplussed. He gazed at Kitty Bridges in slack-jawed shock, trying - and failing - to calculate how much it might have cost to travel by cab from London to Norfolk.

'I can give you a lift back tomorrow,' he said hopefully. He was already imagining Kitty Bridges in the passenger seat of the Opel Manta, laughing at his banter as they drove past fields and hedgerows, through green and glorious swathes of English countryside nothing like the bleak wasteland surrounding The Half Man. Perhaps, on the way back, they could stop off at a picturesque pub for a pint and a Ploughman's...

'No need.' Kitty shrugged again. 'I'll just get another cab.'

Vic was trying to take the rebuff in his stride when she flashed him a dazzling smile. He beamed back at her with the blissed-out expression of a true believer who had died and found himself standing at the open gateway to heaven.

'I don't think we've been properly introduced,' she said. 'I'm Kitty Bridges.'

But before Vic could open his mouth to reply, her attention had already shifted away from him.

'Darts! Ooh, I *love* darts!'

Ridley re-entered the bar with two large suitcases which he deposited at the foot of the stairs. 'Perhaps Mr. Rock can take these up to your room.'

'Yeah, right,' said Rock, with the long-suffering look of a man who was growing weary of having to fetch and carry.

'I'll drink to that!' said Griff. While everyone had been distracted by the new arrival, he had been milking the gash in his forearm so that the blood dripped into an empty glass. Now he raised that glass in a toast, quaffed the contents and bared his bloody teeth at the onlookers.

Vic felt his stomach heave. He looked around the room. Curtis was staring, petrified, at Griff, and Rock's face was thunderous with fury. Ridley was calmly jotting something down in a small notebook, while Kitty was selecting a set of darts from the bar, weighing them thoughtfully in her hands as though they were fresh produce. Noreen, meanwhile, seemed more interested in her white powder. She rolled up a banknote and snorted a line into her left nostril, pinching the right one closed with a gold-tipped finger.

She wiped her nose, looked up and said to Griff, 'Are you serious? Right here? Right now?'

Griff interpreted this as an invitation to misbehave in earnest. 'No time like the present, babe.' He sallied over to the jukebox to choose another record. *Stray Cat Blues* by the Rolling Stones started up, extra vibrato from the heavy sword on the jukebox lending it a sinister metallic undertone.

He began to perform a slow, gyrating striptease.

Vic pretended not to be embarrassed - after all, he was a man of the world - but his gaze drifted from one person to the next, trying to gauge their reactions as he tried hard not to look at Griff peeling off his T-shirt and laying bare a lithe torso covered with a tracery of tattoos, piercings and scars.

He saw Noreen hoovering up another line of white powder, this time into her other nostril.

He saw Curtis quaking like a frightened rabbit.

And he saw Kitty taking aim with one of her darts, and smirked. This was going to be good. She would miss the board by a mile, and that would be his cue to step in and show her how it ought to be done.

Thunk!

Kitty squealed in delight as the dart embedded itself in the triple twenty.

Beginner's luck, thought Vic.

Ridley extended his hand towards Vic, angling his head to indicate the rest of the room. 'Such children. I'm Dr. Magnus Ridley, by the way.'

Vic seized the hand and shook it gratefully, relieved to meet someone halfway normal. 'Vic Pearce. Pleased to meet you, Doctor.'

Thunk!

The noise made him look back at the dartboard, where Kitty's second dart had landed right next to her first, in the triple twenty. Blimey, what were the odds.

'See that?' said Ridley. 'She's good.'

Kitty took aim again.

Thunk!

Vic watched in disbelief as the third dart smacked into the infinitesimal space between its two fellows and sat there, all three fletches quivering in unison.

Kitty began to jump up and down, squealing excitedly. *'One hundred and eighty!'*

Ridley raised an eyebrow '*Very* good.'

Vic barely had time to register this miracle before he was distracted, yet again, by a loud snort from Noreen, who was busily snuffling up another line of white powder. His own nose twitched in empathy. What if he were to casually stroll over to her table? Would she offer him a line? More to the point, would she laugh at another of his jokes?

As if she'd read his thoughts, Noreen got to her feet, dabbing her nostrils daintily as she shimmied back towards him. Vic's heart did a small but pleasurable skip of anticipation. He groped around for something to say that wouldn't emerge as a shameless demand for drugs, and ended up with, 'So, did you all meet each other at the funeral?'

Noreen yawned. 'What a boring question. You'll have to do better than that if you want me to fuck you.'

Vic felt like kicking himself. It was as if she'd been his for the taking, and he'd blown it. Trying to cobble together a gambit to get their conversation back on track, he stared at Griff, who was still gyrating to the music, rotating his hips like a belly dancer. With a sudden convulsive movement, the punk kicked out a leg, sending one of his winklepickers sailing across the room. It bounced off the wall just behind Curtis, who shrank down into his seat as far as he could.

Then, as *Stray Cat Blues* gave way to *Tokoloshe Man* by John Kongos, Griff slowly, tantalisingly, began to unzip his fly.

Noreen cackled. 'Oh no! Here it comes!'

Behind the bar, Rock drew himself up to his full height. 'Sir! This is a family pub!'

Griff turned in a wide circle, peering around the bar, hand shading his eyes, look-out fashion. 'I see no families.' He grinned, as though he'd just told a grand joke, inserted his thumbs beneath the waistband of his trousers and, without pausing in his gyrations, began to work the tight leather down around his hips. He wasn't wearing underpants.

Vic didn't know where to look.

Kitty giggled and pretended to cover her eyes, though she was secretly peeking through her fingers as Griff's prominent Prince Albert piercing came into view.

The temperature in the bar suddenly dropped. Vic looked over to the open cellar door, where Mrs. Rock was standing in with a case of wine, cold air blowing in all around her. She was staring wide-eyed at the nearly naked man, her face frozen in shock. Vic saw her stagger, and darted forward to grab the wine before she could drop it. He set the case down on the floor by the bar and closed the cellar door before returning to his seat, hoping Noreen or Kitty had noticed his gentlemanly gesture.

But Noreen and Kitty were too busy watching Griff, now strutting back and forth like a funky chicken. He dipped his finger into the gash in his arm and used the blood as ink, daubing crude symbols over his face and torso. And all the while he was dancing in a circle, chanting in an eerie monotone.

'Ulalume ulalume ulalume!'

'Griff, baby!' cajoled Noreen. 'Are you sure you want to do this right now? You wouldn't like a couple of drinks inside you first?'

Griff ignored her, and continued his chant.

'Arata-te arata-te arata-te!'

Tokoloshe Man faded away and was replaced by the sound of a rushing wind, intermingled with the cawing of crows.

'Ulalume ulalume ulalume!'

Ridley nodded admiringly, and murmured, 'Aromanian *and* Poe. Have to give him credit for that.'

'He's nothing if not original,' said Noreen.

'What the fuck,' said Vic.

Griff's chanting turned into a shout.

'*Arata-te arata-te arata-te!*'

The walls of the bar rippled and sighed. The building itself seemed to be breathing. Mrs. Rock, pale as death, swayed and clutched at the bar as though she were about to faint, or throw up, or maybe both at once. Her husband, a look of absolute horror on his face, groped for the optics, flooded a wineglass with whisky and downed it in one gulp. Kitty sat down abruptly, clutching her head in both hands, as though she could feel a migraine coming on.

Vic didn't feel so great himself. The air was pulsing. Something was about to happen. He had no idea what, but Ridley and Noreen seemed to be expecting it. And Griff himself was smiling at the ceiling, arms outstretched as though calling something down from above.

There was a silence that seemed to last several years, but which was probably more a matter of milliseconds.

First to snap out of the collective stupor was Curtis, who sent his stool flying with a crash. The others watched in astonishment as he flung himself across the room to snatch up the cranial glaive from the jukebox. Face twisted in determination, he tottered beneath its

weight before retrieving his balance, and with a shriek of
'Demon! I defy you!', swung the sword in a square drive,
less like a samurai and more like a batsman hitting a six.
The stroke itself didn't do the damage, but the follow-
through sliced cleanly through Griff's neck.

A geyser of scarlet sprayed an exponential curve
across the wall as the head sailed through the air in a
graceful arc and landed in Vic's lap.

Vic, stunned, stared down at it. *No,* he thought.
This isn't happening. The head blinked up at him, once,
twice. The lips peeled back into one final grimace.

There was a shocked silence, abruptly ripped
apart by Kitty's screams.

It was the cue for everyone to leap to their feet.
Vic straightened up with a convulsive movement more
instinctive than intentional. The head tumbled from his
lap, leaving a rust-coloured stain on his trousers, and
rolled across the floor.

'Jesus fucking Christ,' said Vic.

'Bloody hell,' said Noreen.

'We don't need this,' sighed Ridley.

Rock turned and silently vomited into the sink
behind the bar. His wife bunched her hands into fists
and pressed them over her mouth.

The least flustered person in the room was Brian
Curtis, oblivious to the blood dripping off his face. 'It's
all right, everyone. Stay calm. I can explain everything.'

He raised his arm in what was probably intended
as a reassuring gesture, apparently forgetting he was
clutching a bloodstained sword and standing over the
headless corpse of the man he'd just decapitated.

Vic and Ridley exchanged a look. As one, they
advanced on Curtis and easily disarmed him. Ridley

dropped the glaive on the floor and pinned one of Curtis's arms behind his back; Vic kicked the weapon across the floor, out of reach, and grabbed the other arm.

'Call the police,' said Ridley.

Rock crossed to the phone on the wall. He picked up the receiver and shakily started to dial. 'Can you keep it down?' he said to Kitty, who was still screaming. 'I can't hear myself think.'

Ridley relinquished his hold on Curtis, reached Kitty in two strides and slapped her. She promptly stopped screaming and stood there staring at the headless corpse, unable to wrench her gaze away from the blood pooling on the floor.

Rock got through to the station and tried to describe what had happened. Even though Vic had seen it with his own eyes, the account sounded absurd to his ears. The police would think it was some sort of prank. He felt his entrails twist. Or maybe they'd just pin the blame on him; it wouldn't be the first time he'd been played as a stooge. His mind raced. He wondered if he could skip off before the cops turned up. But where could he spend the night? He still had to talk to Mrs. Saxby in the morning. He couldn't possibly return to Turlingham empty-handed, and this part of the world didn't offer much in the way of accommodation. Lumpy as the bed in his upstairs room was, it was better than dossing down in the Opel.

Noreen dipped down to pick up Griff's head and began to smooth its hair.

'Put that down,' said Rock. 'It's evidence.'

'Of what?' said Noreen. 'This isn't exactly an Agatha Christie situation. There's no mystery here. We all saw what happened.'

Vic supposed she had a point. Even so, he was a little perturbed by the way she was so casually handling the dripping head, as though it were some sort of bowling bowl. It wasn't the first time he'd seen a dead body, but he couldn't imagine any of the women he'd left behind in London acting with Noreen's insouciance. They would have run screaming out of the room.

Still gripping Curtis's arm, he asked Ridley, 'What shall we do with this one?'

Mr. Rock hung up the phone. 'You could lock him in the cellar till the police arrive.'

Curtis said cheerfully, 'No need to worry on my account. I've done what I came here to do. I'm not going to hurt anyone else.'

'Shut it,' said Vic.

Rock opened the cellar door, letting in another blast of freezing air, and flicked a switch so the light came on, showing the steps leading downwards. Ridley and Vic manoeuvred Curtis through the doorway. He turned back to protest again. 'No really, it's all right now. You don't need to...' But Ridley slammed the door on him. Rock turned the key, and slid the bolts across, top and bottom. Curtis's babbling was still audible, but muted by a layer of thick oak.

'I'm not dangerous, you know. I'm not going to kill anyone else.'

'Little turd,' said Ridley, wiping his hands on Rock's teatowel. 'He has no idea what he's done.'

'It's like a fridge in there,' said Vic.

'He can catch his death for all I care,' said Rock. 'But if it makes you feel better, I'll chuck him a blanket.'

'I'd leave the little runt to freeze,' said Ridley.

Vic looked down at the headless corpse with distaste. 'What'll we do with this?'

'Better not touch it,' said Rock.

Kitty stamped her foot. 'I'm not staying here another second with this... *thing* lying there.'

'Put a cork in it, lady,' said Noreen. 'We've all seen worse.'

'*You* might have,' said Kitty. '*I* haven't!'

'I bet you have, you know,' Noreen said, fixing her with a curiously penetrating gaze. 'But you probably don't remember.'

She seemed about to say something else, but Ridley cut in with, 'Now, girls. That's enough, Noreen.'

'We could put it in the taproom,' said Rock, indicating a door in an alcove at the bottom of the staircase. He led the way as Ridley and Vic lugged Griff's headless corpse across the floor, leaving a dribble of blood like a trail of gory breadcrumbs in their wake. Noreen, still holding the head, brought up the rear, like the mourner-in-chief in a funeral procession.

As Rock opened the door, they were met by the reek of stale beer. The taproom was little more than a large cupboard without windows, lined with barrels and crates. Wedged into the remaining space was a trestle table piled with empty beer cans, accounts and invoices. Ridley swept them to the floor with his elbow, and they hefted the headless corpse on to the table.

The doctor nodded to Noreen. 'You can put that down now.' Vic watched in disbelief as she raised the head and planted a lingering kiss on the dead lips, seeming not to mind the blood trickling down her arms. What kind of woman was this? He'd never met anyone like her before. She frightened him, but, at the same time he wanted her, badly.

When Noreen had judged her farewell sufficient, she placed the head on the table, positioning it so the sliced neck matched up perfectly with the body.

'Good night, sweet Griff.'

As soon as she loosened her grip, the head rolled sideways so that its dead gaze seemed to be fixed on Vic. He was relieved when Rock covered the body with a grubby dust sheet. No sooner had the fabric settled than blood began to soak through the upper end.

Ridley and Rock went off to wash their hands, leaving Vic and Noreen on their own. He eyed her warily. 'Sorry about your friend.'

'Oh, you know,' said Noreen, airily waving her blood-streaked fingers. 'You win some, you lose some.'

Once again, Vic was taken aback by her attitude. 'You don't seem very upset.'

'I'm in shock.' Noreen winked at him. 'But it's his own fault. He should have waited.'

'Waited for what?'

'Until all the pieces are in place on the board.'

Vic was growing impatient with her enigmatic utterances. 'He was your bloke!'

'He was my *dealer*,' said Noreen. Her eyes took on a faraway look. 'Though we did once swim the Hellespont together.'

'Hell's what?' said Vic, and gave up, turning to the door. 'Christ, I need a drink.'

CHAPTER 4: SWEET DREAMS

Vic went behind the bar and poured generous Single Malts for himself and Noreen. No-one stopped him, nor did anyone seem to be keeping a tab, least of all the Rocks. Still, he thought, drinks should be on the house considering all the shit that was happening. Mr. Rock was already cradling his own generous whisky, leaving his wife busy with a mop and bucket.

'When will the cops be here?' asked Vic, secretly thankful they hadn't yet turned up. He needed to think carefully about his story. Probably best not to mention Turlingham. He wondered if there was a computer at the station. He hoped not. Last thing he needed was them looking up his record.

'Not until the morning,' said Mr. Rock.

'Nice to know they're speeding to our rescue,' said Kitty, who seemed to have recovered from her shock and was now on her second glass of Asti Spumante. 'Can't they get here any earlier than that?'

'High tide,' said Rock. 'Flash flooding along the coast road. Happens all the time around here.'

'Lovely part of the world,' said Vic. He gestured with his thumb at the cellar door. 'Who is this geek, anyway? Anyone know him?'

'A nobody,' said Noreen. 'We just met him today, same as you.'

Ridley was drinking a clear liquid that might have been vodka. 'You may think he's a nobody, my dear, but I intend to take a closer look at Brian Curtis's effects.'

65

'Good idea,' said Vic. 'Which room was he in?'

Rock, bleary-eyed, selected a key from behind the bar and dropped it into Vic's hand. 'Third on the right, past the bathroom. Be my guest. Sacrificed his right to privacy when he turned my bar into an abattoir.'

Vic grabbed his Single Malt and made for the staircase, followed by Ridley and Noreen.

'Wait for me,' said Kitty, picking up her glass. 'I'm not staying in this creepy bar all by myself. Also, can someone bring up my luggage?'

*****

The floorboards popped and crackled beneath their feet as Ridley, Vic and Noreen crossed the landing, Kitty bringing up the rear.

'Which room?' asked Ridley, opening the first door on the left.

'That's mine,' said Vic.

Noreen smiled at him. 'Mine's the last on the left.' She nodded towards the picture window at the end of the passage. Vic was uncomfortably aware she hadn't bothered to wash the blood off her hands. The thought made him hard, and also a little queasy.

Ridley scanned the cramped interior of Vic's room with a neutral expression before closing the door. 'If I were you I would keep this locked,' he said to Vic.

'Yeah, starting to think that's not a bad idea,' said Vic. He and Ridley deposited Kitty's luggage in her room, which looked bigger and more comfortable than Vic's. Then Vic inserted the key into the lock on Curtis's door. 'Geek was in here.'

He stepped into Brian Curtis's room. It was almost identical to his own: same narrow bed, faded watercolours, rickety chest of drawers and wardrobe. But the window looked out on to the endless marshes behind the inn, a view even darker and more dispiriting than Vic's.

Ridley picked up an orange nylon holdall and wrenched it open. Noreen lounged in the doorway, smoking, while Kitty hovered behind her looking disdainful, as though she considered the room too low-rent for her to set foot in.

Ridley extracted the holdall's contents and arranged them on the bed: one toothbrush, one pair of pyjamas, one clean pair of underpants, five notebooks, a snarl of rosaries, knobs of garlic, a faggot of sharpened stakes, one mallet, one map of Prague, three rolls of parchment, one buff-coloured file and a dog-eared teddy bear.

Noreen swooped on the teddy. 'Well hello, Mr. Bear.'

Vic shot her an amused glance. 'Like soft toys, do you?'

'I prefer hard ones,' said Noreen.

Ridley seemed irritated by their banter. 'Stop messing around, you two.' He smoothed out the map - some of the streets were marked in red Biro - and opened the buff-coloured file. A newspaper cutting fell out. Justin Saxby's obituary. Vic started flicking through the notebooks, but they were crammed to the margins with handwriting so constipated that trying to decipher it threatened to give him a headache, so he soon gave up.

67

Noreen unrolled one of the parchments, tilted her head to read something, and whistled through her teeth. 'Look at this.'

Ridley peered over her shoulder. 'My God, I had no idea.'

Vic took a look as well. 'What?' All he could see were acres of markings in an alphabet so foreign he couldn't even pronounce the words. That is, if they *were* words. It might as well have been a diagram of some sort of advanced electrical circuit.

'It seems our mad friend is quite the classical scholar,' said Ridley. 'Look at this cuneiform, and this Sanskrit here. Not bad, not bad at all.'

'Hmm,' said Noreen. 'A little sloppy in the syntax, if you ask me.'

'And his punctuation's all over the shop,' quipped Vic. It was only when Ridley and Noreen frowned back at him that he realised they'd been speaking in earnest. *Bloody intellectuals*, he thought.

Ridley picked up the file and the notebooks. 'Bedtime reading. You two should get some sleep.'

'What about me?' Kitty called from the corridor.

'You too, Miss Bridges,' said Ridley. 'We're in for a long day tomorrow.'

'Not me,' Vic muttered under his breath. He was still planning to visit Mrs. Saxby first thing in the morning. He would get her to sign the papers, then grab whatever it was Turlingham wanted, and head for home just as soon as he could. If the cops wanted a statement they would have to track him down in London. He had no intention of hanging around this godforsaken dump any longer than was necessary.

As he turned to follow Ridley out of the room, Noreen blocked the doorway.

'I'm so frightened,' she said, not looking frightened in the least.

On the other hand, thought Vic, the godforsaken dump did have its compensations.

Ridley turned and tutted. 'Noreen! Let Mr. Pearce get some rest. He's had a long and difficult journey.'

'No, I haven't,' said Vic, but it was too late. Noreen was already backing down the corridor towards her door. She blew him a kiss.

'Sweet dreams, Mr. Pearce. I do hope we can get together tomorrow.'

'Same here,' said Vic, feeling torn. Maybe he could put off his departure for a few hours... He'd never met anyone quite like Noreen before. Perhaps he could talk her into giving him her telephone number.

*****

Vic's dreams were anything but sweet.

To the click-clack rhythm of Newton's Cradle, the cranial glaive whistled through the air in a mighty arc. A long way off at first, but coming closer, and closer, and closer... Swish... Swish... Swish... Like a giant pendulum.

Vic backed away from it till he could go no further, and then the glaive was *there*. He felt the sting as the blade sliced through his neck, and watched the room turning round and round as his head flew through the air.

Blood splashed the walls.

His head landed in Noreen's lap. She picked it up. Vic felt her lips clamped to his, hungrily kissing him, licking him, until... Her tongue emerged from her mouth, longer and longer, until it was burrowing into his throat and emerging from the back of his cranium...

Kitty screamed, on and on, in an impossibly high voice that hurt his ears. She was tied naked to a table, surrounded by cowled figures and struggling to tear herself free. Vic's headless torso stepped forward to untie her, but at the last moment, one of the figures thrust a knife into its hands. His disembodied head screamed no, but he was unable to stop his arms from raising the knife over her squirming body.

'Now!' said one of the figures, lowering its cowl so Vic could see its face. It was Turlingham! And it wasn't Kitty tied to the table but Diane. No, not Diane. It was...

Vic watched helplessly as the blade plunged down towards his own torso.

Vic's eyes snapped open. He was sprawled across the narrow bed, sweating like a porker, tangled in muggy sheets and with an erection that was threatening to erupt out of his Y-fronts. He stared dully at the unfamiliar ceiling. It was a long and disorientating moment before he was able to work out where he was, but then the events of the previous evening came back to him in a rush. Little wonder he'd had nightmares.

He sat up and lit a cigarette. The bad dream was already slipping away from him, which was a mercy, because it had been a humdinger. He got off the bed, naked except for the underpants. If only he'd thought to bring a spare pair, like Brian Curtis. Maybe he could sneak back into the nerd's room and nick that clean pair while no-one was looking. On the other hand, he was a lot bigger than Curtis, and he wasn't sure he wanted any item of that creep's clothing in such close proximity to his private parts.

He padded over to the window to gaze at the unending marshlands with their flat and sinister gleam. The moon was a big one, almost full, but the light it cast was like the glow of something pale that dwelt deep within the earth.

Nothing was moving out there. Nothing alive, at any rate...

But, deep in the bowels of the Half Man, something stirred.

Vic's ears pricked up as they picked up unfamiliar sounds: the faint rattle of something metallic, a guttural moaning that may or may not have been the wind, the shuffling of rotting footsteps on the staircase, climbing slowly, coming closer, scraping and shuffling...

It was the headless corpse!

He tried to suppress the thought. Of course it wasn't the headless corpse. That was ridiculous. It was probably just the ancient building adjusting to changes in air pressure...

The floorboards on the landing creaked.

Vic turned slowly to face the door.

Something was scratching at the other side.

He watched, feeling his hair literally standing on end as he saw the handle turn... The door rattled on its hinges but didn't open. He thanked his fairy godmother he'd followed Ridley's advice and locked it.

In a quavering voice he said, 'Noreen? Is that you?'

No answer. Just more metallic scraping, and a faint scrabbling, as though there was a large dog outside, clawing at the door, wanting to come in.

The handle turned again.

'Fuck off,' said Vic, too softly for anyone outside to hear.

Silence. He realised he'd been holding his breath and let it out, but even as he did so he could hear a distant howling. Did they have wolves out here in Norfolk? And what was that other noise? Surely it couldn't be... sobbing?

The scrabbling and howling and sobbing merged, and soared in a heartstopping crescendo. Vic covered his ears with his hands.

'I'm not scared. I'm *Victor Ignatius Pearce*. People are scared of *me*.'

And then it was quiet again.

Vic lit another cigarette. He noticed his hands were trembling.

Those noises had been the ancient plumbing, he told himself. His own radiators back home didn't half make a racket starting up.

Or maybe he'd been dreaming again. His imagination was working overtime, and maybe he'd inadvertently carried some of the dream back into the room with him.

In any case, it was quiet now, and that was all that mattered.

Tomorrow he would be out of here.

He finished his cigarette and climbed back into bed. He had little desire to go back to sleep, but all the same he drifted off, and the bad dreams reclaimed him.

CHAPTER 5: THE INSPECTOR

Mrs. Rock placed a large plate of fried eggs and fatty bacon on the table. Vic stared down at the food and felt his stomach heave.

She hovered over him solicitously. 'Tea or coffee?'

He turned his pink and bleary eyes up at her. 'Got any Alka-Seltzer?'

She smiled a thin-lipped smile. 'Of course. My husband always has a plentiful supply.' She wiped her hands on her soiled apron and moved off, returning a few minutes later with a glass of busily fizzing water.

Vic sipped at it cautiously. More to avert his eyes from the greasy eggs and bacon than out of any genuine curiosity, he leant back in his chair, lit a cigarette, and surveyed the bar.

On the other side of the room, Kitty was showing every sign of having recovered from her ordeal of the previous evening. She was perched on the edge of a table, emitting delighted little squeals of laughter, tossing her hair, and showing lots of leg for the benefit of the two uniformed policemen who were gazing at her in rapture, besotted with this fabulous vision of cosmopolitan pulchritude that had miraculously appeared in front of them.

Vic, whose life experience to date had resulted in automatic distrust of all members of law enforcement, eyed the cops warily, but they were giving no signs of having noticed him. Their attention was too firmly fixed on the blonde.

'It was horrible,' said Kitty. 'So much blood!'

'It's all right, love. We're here now,' said the older of the cops, a pleasant-faced man in his forties.

His younger colleague craned his neck towards Mr. Rock, who was stationed behind the bar, glumly polishing glasses, and waved his empty coffee cup. 'Any chance of a top-up?'

Rock picked up the cafetière and came over to refill the policemen's cups.

'I'll have some of that,' said Vic.

Rock nodded curtly and made a detour on his way back to the bar to fill Vic's cup. Alerted to Vic's presence, the younger cop looked round at last.

'Here's another one who looks like he didn't sleep a wink.'

Vic sipped his coffee and grimaced, as much from having attracted the policeman's attention as from the bitter taste.

'Of course not,' said Kitty. 'None of us could sleep! Not after what happened, Constable Fry. I simply won't feel safe till that madman is behind bars.'

She snuggled up to the younger cop, whose eyes looked as though they were about to pop out of his head at the physical contact. He was behaving like a gauche schoolboy who'd never seen an attractive young woman before, thought Vic. Then again, there probably weren't many women like Kitty Bridges in this neck of the woods. They were probably all old, like Mrs. Saxby, or dour, like Mrs. Rock.

The older cop attempted to reclaim Kitty's attention with a potted summary of the situation, as though he fancied himself as Hercule Poirot. 'Well, we've got a madman in the cellar and a headless corpse in the taproom. Looks like an open and shut case to me.'

Fry countered with, 'But it might have been better if you lot hadn't moved the body... Isn't that right, Inspector French?'

Vic looked round to see who Fry had been addressing, and, for the first time, noticed the man standing in the open doorway of the taproom. How in hell hadn't he noticed him earlier? It wasn't as though this fellow was a shrinking violet, even though he had his back to the bar. You could tell by his clothes: he was wearing a navy blue cashmere overcoat and fancy brogues, which immediately put Vic on his guard. He wasn't used to seeing cops dressed so flashily, not unless they were on the take.

The man in the cashmere overcoat turned to face the bar, and said, 'Who gives a fuck if the body's been moved? We all know who the murderer is.'

Vic stared in astonishment at Detective Inspector French, who was like no cop he'd ever met, and he'd met more than a few, in his time. There was nothing remotely average about this man. He was far too good-looking and well turned out - tall, sleek and dashing, with a haircut so sharp you could have slashed your wrists on it.

French gave Vic an almost imperceptible nod, as if to say *Yes I know I'm not like the others.* In a sequence of movements so elegant and streamlined they might have been rehearsed, he placed a maize-coloured Boyard between his lips, flicked the wheel on an antique brass Zippo and tilted his head to apply the flame to the end of the cigarette. He slowly breathed in a lungful of smoke, savouring the sensation like an oenophile rolling a mouthful of Mouton-Rothschild around his palate, while his sharp green eyes roved keenly around the bar, drinking in every detail.

When he'd taken it all in, his gaze came back to rest on Vic, who shifted uncomfortably in his seat, as he always did when the law looked in his direction.

'Mr. Pearce, I presume? Glad you could join us. Fry, take a statement from our friend here... After he's finished his breakfast, of course.'

The undercurrent of mockery in the detective's words put Vic even more on his guard. He sighed and pushed his untouched plate away. 'Lost my appetite. Let's get this over with.'

Fry reluctantly extricated himself from Kitty's attentions. He came over to sit at Vic's table, extracted a notebook and Biro from one of his pockets and looked up at him inquiringly.

But Vic was still keeping a wary eye on French, as the Inspector sauntered over to the locked cellar door and rapped sharply on it.

'Hello? Hello? Still with us?'

From the other side of the door came the shuffling of footsteps on stone, and muffled groaning.

'Sleep well, Mr. Curtis?' the detective asked jovially.

'It's all right,' said Curtis, his voice sounding incongruously perky considering he'd spent the night in a freezing cellar. 'You can let me out now.'

French shook his head. 'I think not.'

'The danger has passed,' said Curtis's voice.

'Oh, really?'

'I'm not going to kill anyone else.'

76

'You don't say,' said French.

'I've done what I came here to do.'

French raised an eyebrow, playing to the room. 'I'll be the judge of that. Don't go away, Mr. Curtis. We'll get round to you later.'

He pointed at Kitty, who was still making eyes at the older of the cops. 'Miss Bridges. A word with you in private. If you can bear to tear yourself away from Sergeant Wheeler, that is.' He stubbed his Boyard out in the nearest ashtray and crossed to the window.

A change came over Kitty's face, as though the sun had gone behind a cloud. Every last trace of coquetry vanished. She immediately got to her feet and trotted over to join the Inspector.

When Vic had finished giving Fry the blandest, least incriminating statement he could muster, he looked over at French and Kitty and was surprised to see them huddled together, like bosom buddies. French seemed to be whispering into her ear, his hand placed almost proprietorially on the nape of her lovely neck.

Vic thought it odd. If he hadn't known better he might have thought French was sticking his tongue in Kitty's ear... But no, that was impossible. They'd only just met.

*****

The bleakness of the landscape was relieved only by a scattering of twisted trees silhouetted against the sea fog.

Ridley was jogging along in a tidy grey tracksuit, checking his progress now and again on his Rolex Oyster Perpetual with its Paraflex shock absorber.

Despite the muddy track, his sneakers were a dazzling white, as though he'd just coated them in Tipp-Ex.

The jagged outline of the Half Man emerged from the mist up ahead. As soon as he spotted his destination, Ridley burst into a sprint.

There was a rumble of thunder and it began to spit with rain.

When he drew level with the Mercedes, he slowed down again. Parked on the other side was a police car. And sprawled nonchalantly on its bonnet, like an odalisque reclining on a chaise longue, was Noreen, wreathed in sea mist and cigarette smoke.

Ridley jogged on the spot. He was barely out of breath.

'Glad to see you're still watching your figure, Doc,' said Noreen.

'Noreen. What are you doing up before noon?'

Noreen patted the blue light. 'Look who's here.'

'Response time leaves something to be desired,' said Ridley.

Noreen was bursting to share a juicy gossip item. She leant forward eagerly. 'You'll never guess who's joined us.'

Ridley stopped jogging.

*****

The storm beat down on the roof of The Half Man. It rattled the doors, plucked at the chimneys, tugged at the frames and rafters. Gale-force wind, unchecked by the flat landscape, slammed sheets of rain against the windows. With each clap of thunder, the foundations of the building shuddered, the creaking of ancient timbers making the occupants feel as though they were on board a rickety ship, buffeted by the angry swell of the ocean.

Under the circumstances, the bar seemed the safest place. One by one, the guests sauntered down from their rooms, trying to give the impression they were taking the extreme weather in their stride. Curtis and Mrs. Rock were the only absentees; Curtis was still locked in the cellar, and Vic had last seen Mrs. Rock on her knees in the bathroom, scrubbing the floor. Like her husband, she seemed to enjoy cleaning floors.

In the bar, Mr. Rock seemed out of sorts and was prowling around nervously. Ridley had assumed bar duties in his place, and was serving drinks with brisk efficiency. The lights flickered. Crackles of lightning sporadically lit the room.

Vic too was affecting a nonchalance he didn't feel. He'd seen storms before, but never one like this. He felt grateful for the Single Malt suffusing his bones with warmth, a pleasant distraction from the elemental pyrotechnics even if it was a bit early to start on the booze. He just hoped the thunder and lightning cleared up before he had to go and see Mrs. Saxby. He didn't fancy having to drive through this deluge. As it was, the Opel's superannuated windscreen wipers had trouble coping with regular rain.

Noreen, also drinking whisky, was another agreeable distraction. Fry and his colleague, Wheeler, were dutifully sticking to cups of tea. Wheeler kept checking his watch. Rock peered out of the window.

'It's pissing down,' he observed, as though it might have slipped everyone's attention.

French shivered, despite his cashmere coat.

'I don't know how you people can stand this weather. So chilly and wet.'

'Thought you liked storms, Inspector,' said Noreen.

French grimaced. 'So I do. If it's lightning over the Lagoon, viewed while sipping a Bellini cocktail.' He looked hopefully at Mr. Rock. 'I don't suppose you've got any peach purée?'

'Might have some tinned grapefruit slices in the pantry,' said Mr. Rock. 'You want me to go and dig them out?'

French quivered with distaste. 'Forget it.'

'Thirsty, Inspector?' Ridley asked with a cordial smile.

'Always.' French smiled back at him, equally cordial.

It was obvious to Vic that they loathed each other.

Ridley filled a glass with tap water and handed it to Noreen, who swivelled gracefully to present it to French. He took it, sniffed the contents suspiciously, and thrust it back at her in disgust.

'Never touch the stuff. Fish fuck in it, apparently. I'd prefer some of that whisky. Neat, if you please.'

'Of course,' said Ridley, pouring out a measure and picking up the tongs.

'Neat,' repeated French. 'No ice.'

'Silly me,' said Ridley, setting the tongs back down. Vic was surprised he'd even considered it. Only philistines put ice in their whisky.

Just five minutes later, French had somehow contrived to rearrange the bar furniture so he was right at the centre, holding court over the assembled company like Judge Danforth in *The Crucible*. Vic only half-listened as he spun elaborate anecdotes about criminal cases he had cracked, and which all seemed to cast him in the role of a latterday Sherlock Holmes. He even claimed to have dispatched one particularly belligerent criminal with a swordstick. He would have been having a whale of a time had it not been for his subordinates' pedantic insistence on following procedure.

Wheeler was still regularly checking his watch. 'Meat wagon should have arrived by now.'

Ridley emerged from behind the bar and planted himself between Vic and Noreen, trying in vain to waft their cigarette smoke out of his face.

'What, no back-up, Constable?'

Fry turned to French. 'I thought you said reinforcements were on their way. This is a major crime scene.'

Wheeler took out his mobile phone. 'I'll call the station.'

'No use,' sighed Kitty. 'It's a dead spot.'

Wheeler persisted anyway, wandering around the room, trying to get a signal. In vain.

'Try the land line,' said Ridley. 'See what happens.'

'Good idea,' said Wheeler, crossing to the bar phone on the wall.

French was visibly irritated by all this fruitless scurrying. 'Relax, gentlemen. It's all under control.'

Wheeler picked up the receiver and dialled. 'Hello? Hello? Is that you, Lorraine? Can you hear me? Yes. Wheeler... Could you repeat that? Sorry, terrible line. I just wanted to...'

81

'Oh, for fuck's sake,' said French and flicked his Zippo. At that same instant, the bar was lit up by another flash of lightning, followed almost immediately by a stomach-churning rumble of thunder.

Wheeler stared in astonishment at the receiver in his hand.

'It's gone dead.'

French lazily inhaled the smoke from his cigarette and smiled.

Ridley and Noreen exchanged glances.

'Well, fancy that,' said Ridley.

'Must be the storm,' said Noreen.

Fry got to his feet. 'No worries. I'll radio from the car.'

'Why don't you do that, Constable,' said French. 'Oh, and pick up my galoshes while you're there.'

'Will do, sir,' said Fry. He opened the door and, bracing himself against the driving rain, stepped outside.

Vic rose and started to follow, but French blocked his route.

'Where do you think you're going, Mr. Pearce?'

'Business with Mrs. Saxby,' said Vic. 'Then I'll be heading back to civilisation.'

'I'm afraid I can't let you go,' said French. 'Not just yet.'

Vic puffed himself up to his full height. 'I haven't done anything.'

'But you're a witness,' said French.

'I already gave my statement,' said Vic, feeling a sliver of panic at the base of his spine. 'You can't kee...'

The room was seared white by another blinding flash, even more dazzling than the last one. They were still blinking when, milliseconds later, the air itself seemed to split apart with an ear-splitting crash. The window blew inwards in a shower of glass. Years of brawling experience made Vic duck instinctively, just as a smoking chunk of twisted metal whizzed past his head, missing it by inches, and embedded itself, quivering, in the glass front of the jukebox.

There was a stunned pause.

Then, a faint voice from the cellar: 'What's going on?'

Kitty, Ridley and Rock sprinted over to the remains of the window. Wheeler and Noreen ran towards the front door, now hanging off its hinges.

'The fuck?' shouted Vic, rubbing the top of his head in disbelief, his ears ringing like a forty-nine-bell carillon. He stumbled over to join Wheeler and Noreen.

Behind the cellar door, Curtis started yelling incoherently.

French casually stuck another Boyard in his mouth.

In front of the inn, all that remained of the police car was a smoking wreck. The rain hissed and bubbled as it splashed on burning metal. Sizzling debris was strewn far and wide. The Mercedes had born the brunt of the blast; its chassis repurposed into a tropical flower shape. The bonnet of the Morris Minor was bent back like an origami sculpture. Curtis's bike had been folded in two. The only vehicle that appeared to have escaped serious damage was Griff's red convertible.

'My Mercedes,' said Ridley.

'My Manta,' said Vic. One side of the Opel looked as though it had been strafed with a Tommy Gun. Something landed at his feet with a wet thunk. He looked down and saw a severed hand clutching a walkie-talkie.

French strolled across to join them in the doorway and calmly surveyed the mayhem outside.

'Bang go my galoshes,' he said.

*****

The storm simmered down at last, though the rain continued to patter down monotonously. Rock and Ridley fetched armfuls of wood from the shed and started hammering lengths across the shattered window frames, shutting out the last of the half-hearted daylight and casting the already murky bar into full-on Stygian gloom. Mrs. Rock had already wrangled the broken glass into a tidy pile with her broom, and was now mopping up rainwater that had pooled between the flags.

Vic had retreated upstairs. The hammering from the bar was setting him on edge. There was an impressive crack across his window pane, but the glass had held firmer than his nerves, which were shot to pieces. First a decapitation, now an explosion. What the hell had Turlingham got him into? This was worse that the Stratford turf war against the Barnum brothers, and at least back then Vic had known who'd got his back, and who'd been ready to plunge a knife into it. Here, all bets seemed to be off.

He sat on his bed, smoking furiously and shivering in the damp air as he shuffled listlessly through the papers Turlingham had given him. They were covered in endless paragraphs of barely penetrable legalese, full of subheadings and footnotes, with the words CONFIDENTIAL, SAXBY ESTATE and

TURLINGHAM ENTERPRISES prominent at the top of several pages.

He felt the hairs on the back of his neck prickle and glanced up at the mirror on the wall in front of him. When he saw what was reflected there he nearly jumped out of his skin. Amongst the discoloured blotches where the silvering had given out, he could see the door to his room. He could have sworn he'd closed it, but now it was standing open. And leaning against the jamb was Inspector French.

Vic leapt to his feet like a scalded cat, scattering papers off his lap, and whirled round to face the doorway.

'Jesus fucking Christ! How long have you been there?'

French lit a cigarette. 'Seems like forever.'

Unnerved, Vic started to babble. 'That was a fucking bomb, right? Someone planted a fucking bomb in your motor. Who the fuck would do a thing like that?'

French coolly blew out a plume of smoke, which curled like ectoplasm towards the beamed ceiling. 'Quite a lot of outfits I can think of. Terrorists. Criminal masterminds. The mob. The IRA. MI6. The CIA...'

'It's not a laughing matter,' said Vic. 'Two men are dead.'

'What makes you think I'm laughing, Vic? I can call you Vic? And you can call me Mordecai.'

'Mordecai? What kind of fucking name is that?'

French looked amused. 'My late father, rest his horny old soul, had what you might call an erotic fixation on ancient Mesopotamia. But I've been wanting to catch you alone for some time, Vic. You're the only one here I can rely on.'

85

Despite his misgivings, Vic couldn't help feeling flattered.

'What about Dr. Ridley? He seems like a solid enough bloke.'

French shook his head slowly. 'Never trust appearances, Vic. Makes you an easy mark.'

He strolled to the window and looked outside to where Wheeler was picking disconsolately through the wreckage of the police car. Kitty, dressed for the rain in green Barbour jacket and red ankle-boots, was happily splashing through puddles, brandishing a pink umbrella.

French gazed at her paternally. 'Just like a real child.'

'What do you mean?' asked Vic, joining him by the window.

French turned to him. 'Here's the plan, Vic. You go and finish your business with the Widow Saxby as quickly as you can. Then I'll need you back here.'

Vic stuck his chin out. 'I'm going back to London.'

'Ah yes. Mr. Turlingham will no doubt be impatient to see you.'

Vic's mouth fell open. 'You know Turlingham?'

'Friends in low places, Vic.'

Vic decided he might as well come clean. 'I'm supposed to get something for him, but he wouldn't tell me what it was.'

'I don't suppose he knows any more than you do.' French turned to him and grinned, showing two rows of extraordinarily even white teeth. 'But I'm sure you can persuade Mrs. Saxby to tell you, Vic. You can be very... *persuasive*. Or so I've heard.'

Vic shifted uncomfortably. 'She's an old lady.'

86

'But a tricky customer,' said French. 'She can be very tricky, Vic. If you need backup, I'm sure the butler will lend a helping hand.'

'You know Frosty the factotum as well?'

French grinned again. 'Let's just say our paths have crossed.'

'Seems like a lot of crossed paths round here,' said Vic. 'Do *you* know what I'm supposed to be looking for?'

'Not... *precisely*,' said French. 'That's where I'm counting on you.'

Vic felt flattered all over again. This cop trusted him, even if he didn't trust the cop. He'd learned the hard way *never* to trust a cop, and still had the scars to prove it.

'Have you spoken to Mrs. Saxby?' he asked.

'Alas, no. Saxby Hall is... off limits to the force. For the time being, anyway. Justin and Araminta made sure of that.'

'Justin and...?'

'The Saxbys. They've been clever, like Tiger Steele before them.'

'Tiger Steele?' The name rang a bell, but Vic couldn't help feeling out of the loop. His mind was off the leash and racing, but he had no idea where the finishing line was, or even which direction it lay in.

'Old acquaintance, Vic. We've all attended the same social functions at one time or another. But never mind that now. Off you go to Saxby Hall, and I'd like you to drop Sergeant Wheeler off at the crossroads on your way. I'm sending him back to Wells for reinforcements.'

'On foot?'

French shuddered. 'Only way to go in weather like this. Flooding all along the coast. The Saxbys picked their spot, all right. But Wheeler's a local, knows how to get through. Cigarette, Vic?'

Vic cautiously drew one of French's maize-coloured smokes from the case held out to him, lit it and coughed.

French was peering intently into his face.

'Tell me, Vic, what do you think of Miss Duval?'

Vic looked blank.

'Noreen,' prompted French. 'The hot totty with the va-va-voom décolletage. I know she puts lead in your pencil. I've seen the way you look at her.'

'She's charming,' said Vic, though *charming* wasn't exactly the word he had in mind.

'Makes a strong impression, doesn't she?' said French.

Vic nodded assent. 'She certainly does.'

'Don't trust her either,' said French.

*****

The cellar door was open. Mrs. Rock was placing a tray of tea and toast on the top step as Vic came down into the bar with his bag. He shivered.

'Curtis still alive down there?'

She nodded. 'My husband gave him a sleeping-bag.'

'I'd like to settle up,' said Vic.

Mrs. Rock straightened up, looking at him curiously. 'Not staying a second night?'

'No way,' he said. 'Keep it quiet though, will you. French thinks I'm coming back.'

She locked the door and drew the bolts across, pursing her lips. 'He's not the only one. But... as you wish, Mr. Pearce.'

She went behind the bar to get his bill.

*****

It was still bucketing down with rain as Vic inspected the damage to the Opel and concluded, with relief, that it was superficial. But not pretty. Once he got back to London, he would need to take it in to Del's chop-shop for a do-over, which was going to cost him. But at least he wouldn't have to fork out for a whole new motor.

He was about to slide into the driver's seat when he felt a hand on his arm and jumped guiltily.

'Hold on a sec,' said Wheeler.

Vic braced himself. He'd been trying to sneak off without the sergeant, and expected a dressing-down, but the cop just asked him to pop open the bonnet, and walked round to examine the engine before crouching down to inspect the underneath of the chassis as well. Vic realised with a shock that he was checking for bombs.

'Better safe than sorry,' Wheeler said, climbing into the passenger seat. 'Can't be too careful after what happened to Fry. May he rest in peace.'

'More like pieces,' Vic muttered under his breath.

*****

French stood at Vic's bedroom window, smoking and gazing down as the Opel Manta did a three-point turn and set off down the one-track road.

'Catch you later, Vic,' he said.

*****

The Half Man receded into the mist behind them as the car ploughed through the lashing rain. Neither Vic nor Wheeler were natural conversationalists, but Vic made a heroic attempt to chat.

'Sorry about your colleague.'

'Poor bastard,' said Wheeler. 'And I'm the unlucky sod who's gonna have to break the news to his wife and kiddies.'

'Who do *you* think planted the bomb?'

'Fuck knows,' said Wheeler. He fell silent for a bit before speaking up again. 'But wouldn't surprise me if that bastard Rock had something to do with it. Serious gambling habit and ugly drunk, up to his eyeballs in debt only a few years ago. We had to deal with some rather nasty characters around these parts. And there were rumours he used to beat his wife.'

Vic remember Mrs. Rock's dour expression. 'But he stopped?'

'Well, of course,' said Wheeler, looking slightly askance. 'But there's still something rum about that fellow, and I intend to find out what it is. I owe it to Fry.'

'You knew him well?'

'Few years,' said Wheeler. 'Weren't exactly best mates, though we downed the odd pint together. Was a good lad. Didn't deserve to go out that way.'

He seemed close to tears, so Vic swiftly changed the subject.

'How about Inspector French? How long have you known him?'

Wheeler made a clucking noise through his teeth. 'About six hours. Special branch. Up from fucking London. What a wanker, eh? Thinks he knows it all.'

Vic wanted to ask more questions about French, but Wheeler was already squinting out of the side window. The rain had veiled the crossroads until now they were almost on top of it.

'This is where I get out. Thanks for the lift. Oh, and Pearce...'

Vic tensed.

'I'd watch your back if I were you.'

'Thanks,' said Vic. 'I intend to.'

A wooden signpost pointed the way to Wells and, in the opposite direction, Saxby Hall. Vic couldn't remember having passed the post the day before, but Wheeler seemed to know where they were. He got out of the car and, tugging his collar up around his neck, turned his back on the signpost and began to splash off along an unmarked track.

Vic leant out of the window to shout after him. 'Thought you were going to Wells!'

'Coast path's quicker!' Wheeler yelled back at him. 'Back in a couple of hours with the cavalry. Have my pint waiting!'

Vic shouted again: 'Forget the pint, mate. I'd rather stick needles in my eyes than go back to that fucking dump.'

But the policeman was already out of earshot. It took only a few more seconds for his hunched figure to be completely swallowed up by the fog and the rain.

91

*****

The remains of Constable Fry had been rounded up and placed in a cooler bag, which had in turn been placed in the pantry with a handwritten notice stapled to it: POLICE EVIDENCE DO NOT TOUCH.

Mr. Rock had managed to set the front door back on its hinges, albeit precariously, and with the help of some strategically placed nails. French carefully closed it and turned to face Ridley, who'd installed himself on a stool, his back against the bar.

The two of them were alone. From upstairs came the steady drumbeat of hammering as the Rocks boarded up the last of the broken windows.

'Now then, Doctor,' said French.

'Long time, no see,' said Ridley.

French went behind the bar and helped himself to a large whisky from one of the optics. 'Can I get you anything?'

Ridley smiled coldly. 'Kind of you to offer, *Inspector*. But, like you, I watch what I drink.'

He reached around to help himself to a bottle of lager, popping the cap off on the edge of the bar.

CHAPTER 6: THE WIDOW

'You surely can't expect me to sign it over to Mr. Turlingham just like that, even if he was once kind enough to lend us a great deal of money.'

Araminta Saxby held out her empty sherry glass. Frost immediately stepped forward to refill it.

She was leafing through the papers Vic had given her, an expression of ineffable disdain on her face. Knowing Turlingham as he did, he couldn't blame her. She was a handsome, intelligent woman whose widow's weeds gave her a formidable air. She was also roaring drunk, though doing a pretty good job of concealing it. She wasn't even slurring her words, though every so often her gaze seemed to wander around the room and alight on something that wasn't there.

They were sitting in the library at Saxby Hall - an imposing gallery cluttered with far too much furniture, crumbling tomes, astrolabes and exotic statuary. Those parts of the wall not occupied by bookshelves were hung with geographical charts and faded photographs of what Vic guessed were the young Saxbys, posing stiffly in pith helmets or Panamas amid dilapidated ruins, standing next to dusty Jeeps or single-engine Austers, or surrounded by archaeological paraphernalia.

Vic was perched on an overstuffed sofa flanked by bow-legged side tables, and he was under siege. Mrs Saxby had ordered her three smelly lurchers - Buffy, Muffy and Slappy - to leave him in peace, but they'd taken absolutely no notice of their mistress and persisted

93

in clambering all over the visitor, drooling and nuzzling his crotch, or intermittently trying to hump his arms and legs. He was growing weary of having to fend them off, but it was either that or end up with visible damp patches on his trousers.

There was a delicate rattle of crockery. He peered around the hairy withers of one of the panting mutts and saw Frost offering him a cup and saucer. Vic accepted them gratefully, took a sip from the cup and tried not to gag. The tea was much too pale, smelled like burnt barbecue, and tasted like a toilet.

This place was almost as creepy as The Half Man, though at least the crackling fire was warming him up after the chilly drive. He felt himself being watched, not just by the widow and her beady-eyed butler, but by the stuffed wildlife scattered around the room, frozen in mid-trot or beheaded and pinned screaming to the wall. He recognised a moth-eaten fox, which looked as though it had probably expired of rabies, but some of the other creatures weren't so easily identifiable. What was that hairy creature with the sharp teeth and horns, for example? And the scaly six-legged beast with the unnaturally long neck?

'I totally understand, ma'am,' he said. 'But I'm just a messenger, so if you'd be so good as to sign these papers, I can take them back to The Smoke as quickly as possible.'

'The Smoke? Is that what they're calling it now?' Mrs. Saxby sounded amused. 'I can tell you, Mr. Pearce, *The Smoke* is what that city will be reduced to, literally, if Turlingham ever gets his hands on what he seeks so urgently. He has no idea what he's dealing with.'

'I have to get going,' said Vic. 'They were expecting me back in town yesterday.'

Mrs. Saxby peered at him over the tops of her spectacle frames, her eyes sparkling and keen. 'You seem inordinately eager to leave us, Mr. Pearce. Our local hostelry not good enough for you?'

'If I never see that dump again, it'll be too soon,' said Vic.

Mrs. Saxby leant towards him. His nose picked up a whiff of peppermint and lavender, a welcome alternative to the odour of damp dog clogging his sinuses.

'Why? Has something happened?'

Vic fumbled for his cigarettes. 'Mind if I smoke?'

'Actually yes, I do mind,' said Mrs. Saxby. 'And you haven't answered my question.'

The trembling in Vic's hand transmitted itself to his cup and saucer, which rattled gently. Where to begin?

'I've seen some stuff in my time, but this takes the biscuit. We had to call the cops.'

Mrs. Saxby sat up straight as a ramrod, a curious gleam in her eye. 'Have you now. I was expecting something of this ilk, but not so soon. Have there already been... casualties?'

'Ye-es,' said Vic. 'Not that anyone seems bothered. They're behaving as though...'

Mrs. Saxby nodded knowingly. 'As though they've seen it all before.' She polished off her sherry in one gulp, and held out her glass for another top-up, but Frost was busy elsewhere, mopping up after the teapot, which had dribbled all over the parquet.

'You probably met them at the funeral,' said Vic. 'They're an odd lot, apart from Dr. Ridley, who seems like a regular sort. But the others... Why would a gentleman like your late husband make friends with people like them?'

'My late husband and I met many unusual people on our travels,' said Mrs. Saxby. 'Not all of them were friends.'

Vic frowned. 'And that Inspector - he has a nasty habit of creeping up on you. He's not like any copper I've ever met. I think he's bent.'

Mrs. Saxby stood up, deposited her empty glass on Frost's tray, and, before Vic could react, was pushing Muffy to the floor and taking the dog's place on the sofa next to Vic. With long and elegant fingers she began to lightly caress his sleeve.

Vic promptly deposited his cup and saucer on the nearest side table and lurched to his feet. Once again he offered his ballpoint pen to Mrs. Saxby, who regally ignored it.

'Please, Mrs. Saxby. Just one signature, and I'll leave you to mourn your late husband in peace.'

Mrs. Saxby snapped her fingers at Frost, who had finished his mopping. He duly furnished her with more sherry. She nodded towards Vic. 'And pour one for our guest. The tea is clearly not to his taste.'

'No, really,' said Vic. 'I've got a long drive ahead.'

'We'll see about that,' said Mrs. Saxby. She tilted her head at him, almost coquettishly. 'Why are you *really* here, Mr. Pearce?'

'I already told you. Turlingham sent me.'

'But why you? Why *you*?'

'Because I was banging his wife and he wanted me out of the way. I'm sorry, I didn't mean to...'

96

'Sit down, young man.' Vic hesitated. She narrowed her eyes and fixed him with a gaze that brooked no refusal. 'I insist.'

Reluctantly, Vic sat back down on the couch, as far from the widow as possible. Buffy enthusiastically resumed his crotch-sniffing. When the old woman got to her feet again, Vic relaxed, only to tense up once more as she stationed herself directly behind him and began to knead his shoulders. Her hands were surprisingly firm, the fingers sinking into his aching muscles and squeezing the stiffness out of them. He squirmed in embarrassment.

'Tell me more about this *Inspector*,' said Mrs. Saxby.

Vic wished he'd had time to quiz Wheeler more thoroughly. 'Mordecai French. Special Branch.'

'Mordecai,' echoed Mrs. Saxby. She abruptly removed her hands from Vic's shoulders, and motioned to her factotum.

'Leave us, Frost. Mr. Pearce and I have private business to discuss.'

'Madam.' Frost bowed stiffly and slipped from the room.

'So you'll sign?' Vic said hopefully.

Mrs. Saxby walked around the sofa to face him. She wasn't tall, but since he was sitting down and she was not, she loomed over him. 'And this Inspector is there now? With Dr. Ridley and his two degenerate companions?'

'Only one companion now. Other one's dead, murdered right in front of us last night. And then one of the cops got blown up this morning. Car bomb.'

97

'Is that so? And who else is staying at The Half Man?'

Vic counted them off on his fingers. 'There's a posh debutante called Kitty Bridges, and a French chick called Noreen Duval. Or maybe she's Irish, or North African, hard to tell. And Mr. and Mrs. Rock, of course. And a madman called Brian Curtis. We had to lock him in the cellar.'

'Brian Curtis is not mad,' said Mrs. Saxby.

'Could have fooled me. He's the one who cut Griff's head off.'

'Well, I'm sure Griff, as you call him, will get over it.'

'Did you hear what I said? *His head was cut off.*'

Mrs. Saxby seemed not to be taking in what Vic was saying. Instead, she toyed with the string of pearls around her neck. 'Mr. and Mrs. Rock, you say. Interesting. Are you certain they're man and wife?'

'They sure act like it. Ignoring each other most of the time.'

Mrs. Saxby looked thoughtful for a moment. Then reared up to her full height. Even old and drunk, she radiated steely willpower.

'The Half Man is an eldritch place. You must not go back there!'

'Suits me,' said Vic. 'I'll be out of here just as soon as you sign...'

Mrs. Saxby snatched up the papers from the side table where she'd left them and with an imperious gesture flung them into the air. They fluttered slowly to the floor like large white leaves.

'I will *not* sign! I will *not* allow this priceless treasure to fall into the hands of a reprobate like

Turlingham. Forget the papers, they are of no importance. I've dealt with his lawyers before, and they are double-dealing charlatans. But you, Mr. Pearce, you must leave right now, this minute. Your life is in danger!'

'It'll be in fucking danger if I go back without your John Hancock,' said Vic, dropping to his knees to retrieve the scattered papers and shuffle them back into some sort of order. It was all going pear-shaped. This old biddy wasn't as senile as he'd expected, but she was stubborn as a mule, which was possibly even worse.

As he reached for a sheet that had landed further away, his shirt untucked itself and rode up, exposing a glimpse of the blue and green scales around his waist. Mrs. Saxby let out a horrified gasp and put out a hand to steady herself against an armchair.

'Where did you get those markings?'

'What?'

'The *tattoo*.'

Vic considered spinning one of his yarns about voyages in exotic lands, but his instinct told him Mrs. Saxby had been around the world, several times, and would know instantly that he'd never been further than Weston-super-Mare.

'Turlingham's stag weekend. Everyone was getting them.'

'Everyone?'

'Yeah. Me. Turlingham. Couple of mates of his. Some businessmen we bumped into. I don't remember too well, to be honest.'

'You don't remember who was there?'

'We were hammered.'

'Hammered?'

'Too much to drink.'

'But some more *hammered* than others, am I right?' asked Mrs. Saxby. 'Did you prepare your own beverages?'

'Course not. What do you think I am, a barman?'

'What *do* you remember of that weekend?'

Vic thought back, not for the first time, but Turlingham's stag party obstinately remained a gaping black hole in his memory. It wasn't the only black hole there, since he'd always had a tendency to overindulge, but it was the only gap that really troubled him. He retained a vague impression of karaoke, but the songs hadn't been in English, and of stripping naked under moonlight, and something happening that had been out of his control, but that was all. The way Turlingham had treated him afterwards had only confirmed his suspicions that he'd disgraced himself, and he'd never wanted to inquire further. Some things it was better not to know.

Mrs. Saxby was still staring at him, but the steely determination in her gaze was now mixed with compassion, which only made him feel more uncomfortable.

'Listen, Mr. Pearce. My late father found something on one of his expeditions, something he learned could bestow unimaginable power on its possessor.'

Her voice was all of a sudden so icy that Vic felt himself break out in goose pimples.

'He didn't want it for himself, but he knew he had to keep it out of the hands of those who would have used it for ill. Later it was stolen from him, but he tracked it down and recovered it - at the cost of his own life. For decades, Justin and I kept it hidden, but we failed to appreciate its true value. We were young and giddy, we lived for the moment, but even in the early days we dared not keep it here, at the house. It was far too dangerous. People came looking for it. And not just people... They're looking for it still, and time is of the essence... Do you understand what I'm talking about?'

'Not really,' said Vic.

'It's in The Half Man!' said Mrs. Saxby, working herself into a froth. 'That's why they're gathering. You think they cared about Justin? They couldn't wait to see him dead! They didn't come here to pay their respects; they came to sniff around his corpse!'

Vic sat back on his heels. He was curious, despite himself.

'What are they looking for?'

'Justin placed a guardian over it,' said Mrs. Saxby. 'But he never told me the details, believing that would protect me. We did that, you know - kept things from each other, secrets that were best not shared lest they be forcibly spilled. All I know is that it's safe - but not for very much longer, not while the moon grows full, not while *you* are still here. Every second counts. You must leave at once!'

She started to pace up and down the room, waving her arms and prodding the charts on the walls with her bony yet elegant fingers as though they held the key to the mystery. The brisk clicking of her heels on the parquet reverberated around the library, bouncing off the ceiling beams. As she paced, her footsteps were echoed by a muffled knocking which reminded Vic of the hammering back at The Half Man. Had the storm broken windows at Saxby Hall as well? Maybe Frost was having to nail boards across the frames.

101

Mrs. Saxby seemed not to notice the sound. She began to rant, and Vic got wearily to his feet, revising his earlier opinion. Clearly her grasp on reality was more tenuous than he'd thought.

'Do you remember Alexandria? Burton and Speke were as pygmies next to you, my darling. Look, Justin, look what we did in Damascus! We went from Cambridge to China, from Mongolia to Norfolk, and they followed us everywhere, everywhere... But they never caught up with us, no, never got their claws on it. We saw to that, didn't we, Justin! But what's going to happen now that you're gone? Listen, there's one of them now!'

She whirled dramatically round to face Vic, who stared back at her in disbelief. The old lady was pointing a revolver at him, holding it steady with both hands.

Christ, she was even nuttier than he'd thought.

Vic half-raised his hands, trying to hold Mrs. Saxby's gaze with his own, and backed carefully away from her, towards the door. Which was easier said than done with Muffy and Slappy winding themselves playfully around his legs.

'Now wait a minute, Mrs. Saxby. I'm sure we can work something out...'

The old lady tilted her head slightly, closed one eye, took careful aim, and squeezed the trigger.

The bullet whizzed past Vic's head. For a moment, the burning sensation made him think she'd taken his ear off. Then the burning subsided, and he heard a groan behind him. He turned just in time to see the thin goon sink to his knees, dropping his cut-throat razor, leaving both hands free to try and stem the blood steadily trickling from the furrow in his neck.

'Fuck me,' said Vic. 'It's Thin Tony!'

'One of Turlingham's?' asked Mrs. Saxby.

Vic nodded. Thin Tony gurgled and tried to say something. Vic strode up to him and kicked him in the ribs. The stricken goon folded up in agony.

'Now, now, Mr. Pearce, we must be civilised,' said Mrs. Saxby, though she didn't sound very upset. Vic felt a new respect for the old lady. Maybe she wasn't as batty as he'd thought. She knew how to handle herself, that was for sure, and he had the impression this wasn't the first time she'd shot somebody.

'You always were... an arsehole... Pearce,' groaned Thin Tony.

Vic gave him one last kick. He picked up the razor, folded it and slipped it into his pocket. The way things were going, he reasoned, it could well come in handy.

'I'm not one for turning the other cheek, and this geezer deserves a good kicking, but seeing as this is your house, Ma'am... Is he going to croak?'

Mrs. Saxby shook her head. 'Unlikely. It's just a scratch. I'll have Frost patch him up. Where is Frost, by the way?'

They found the factotum sprawled in the hallway, moaning and massaging the lump on the back of his head where Thin Tony had coldcocked him.

'Stop lounging around, Frost,' said Mrs. Saxby. 'Come and help me get this scoundrel under lock and key.'

'Certainly Madam,' said Frost, struggling to his feet. 'Did you have anywhere in mind?'

'The laundry room,' said Mrs. Saxby. 'I would have proposed the cellar, but it's knee-deep in water right now, and we wouldn't want this gentleman to catch a cold, even if he did clobber you.'

She looked straight at Vic and gave a start, as though surprised to see him. 'Still here, Mr. Pearce? Go! Go right now, before the weather gets any worse. And it *will* get worse, believe me.'

'But I... But I haven't...' stuttered Vic. He made a move back towards the papers scattered over the carpet, trying to gather as many as he could.

'No buts, young man! Forget your precious papers. Signed or not, they're nothing less than a death warrant. I'm afraid Turlingham has already seen to that. You don't have to go back to London. Go somewhere else! Go anywhere! Catch a plane to Argentina! But you need to get as far away from The Half Man as possible, before it's too late.'

Thin Tony's lips peeled back from bloodstained teeth in a grotesque leer. 'You can run, Pearce, but you can't hide!'

'We'll see about that,' said Vic. 'I'm pretty good at hiding.' He headed for the front door, which was standing ajar, letting in rain.

Mrs. Saxby shouted. Vic turned back, thinking she was calling to him, then realised she was shouting into the air. He shuddered as her voice grew stronger, echoing around the house, and was absorbed into the ancient stones of the mansion.

'Can you hear me, Justin? It's your Minty calling! I love you, you adorable bookworm!'

Frost, still rubbing the back of his head, nodded at Vic. 'If I were you, I'd do as she says. I've seen some rum stuff while I've been working here, I can tell you.

She knows what she's talking about. Get as far away from here as you can.'

Vic didn't need any more telling. As he was pulling the front door shut behind him, he could still hear Mrs. Saxby's voice, which had risen to an unearthly shriek.

'Remember! Remember what you said after Dar Es Salaam, my darling. *Le château brûle, mais il faut cultiver notre jardin! Cultivons notre jardin!*'

Vic didn't speak French, but the words made him shiver all the same.

CHAPTER 7: THE MIST

Vic was chomping at the bit to get away, but the wretched failure of his mission put the kibosh on any feelings of relief he might have entertained, and at the first bend in the driveway, he braked sharply, assailed by second thoughts. He sat with the motor running for a while, wondering whether to nip back and have one last go at securing the old lady's signature.

He turned to look at Saxby Hall, now little more than a smudge on the landscape, nearly lost to view behind a curtain of misty drizzle. The memory of his meeting with Mrs. Saxby was already becoming fuzzy around the edges, as though it had been a dream all along.

No, going back would only be a waste of time. Better to follow the old biddy's advice and get as far away from this freak show as possible.

He set off again, pausing only to open and close the gates, before retracing his route to the crossroads, where he squinted through tendrils of fog at the signpost. Where the hell was he going? London was out of the question now, with Turlingham and his crew waiting for him there. But he didn't fancy Argentina either, not after the Falklands War and Maradona's Hand of God, and anyway he didn't have a passport. Maybe he could stow away on a packet boat?

But first things first: he had to get out of this fog. Maybe visibility would be better further inland. He struck off in the direction of Wells, headlights straining against the swirling mist. He drove for half an hour, until he came to the bridge.

Bridge! What bridge? All that remained of the structure he'd crossed the day before were a few splinters. The chuckling stream had swelled into a raging brown torrent that was threatening to burst its banks.

Vic cursed. He would have to find another way round. He did a six-point turn and headed back to the crossroads. But after forty minutes there was still no trace of that dratted signpost. Instead, he found himself approaching a fork in the road he couldn't recall having seen before. He slowed to a crawl, peering out of the windows in the hope of spotting a landmark, but the landscape was featureless as fresh blotting paper. The rain had petered out, but the air itself was now soggy with moisture, the fog getting thicker by the second.

He was lost.

A large puddle materialised in the road ahead. He thought about trying to drive around it, but the verges on either side looked sodden and treacherous, so he put his foot down and ploughed into the water, relying on speed to carry him across.

Halfway through, he realised to his exasperation that the puddle was deeper than it looked. A *lot* deeper. The car spluttered to a stop. He stamped down hard on the accelerator, but the wheels spun uselessly, mired in mud. He revved the engine, again and again, until it coughed one last time, and died.

He was stuck fast, in the middle of nowhere.

Vic let out a stream of South London vernacular. He opened the door, and a sluggish tide of muddy water flowed in around his ankles. He swore again. He stuffed what he'd managed to retrieve of Turlingham's papers into an inside pocket, grabbed his bag and clambered out. Now up to his knees in mud, he set his shoulder against the car and pushed as hard as he could, but the vehicle refused to budge.

Oh, this was *great*. This was *just* what he needed.

He kicked out furiously at the nearest wheel before wading to firmer land. The only option left was to try and find his way back to Saxby Hall on foot. He peered around, but there was nothing to see, and no help to be had, so with yet another curse, he squelched onwards, further into the fog, which seemed to be deadening all sound except for the eerie muffled cries of seabirds. At least, Vic hoped they were seabirds. He didn't trust his senses any more. After everything that had happened, it wouldn't have surprised him to find he'd travelled back through time into an age ruled by pterodactyls.

After ten minutes of fruitless squelching, the mud threatening to claim his shoes at every step, he spotted the outline of a signpost ahead, and his spirits lifted. He'd made it! Now he could find his way back to Saxby Hall, or even to a main road where he'd be able to hitch a lift.

The fog was so thick he had to walk right up to the sign to read it.

COAST PATH

Vic was disappointed, but not discouraged. It was better than nothing. Was this the route Wheeler had taken? Well, if the copper had found his way out of here, Vic reasoned, so could he. How hard could it be? All he had to do was stick to the path, and he'd be in Wells in no time. Feeling more optimistic, he struck out in the direction indicated by the signpost.

108

He couldn't tell, exactly, when the mud beneath his shoes changed to sand, but walking was becoming increasingly laborious. There was a sound behind him, a weird scraping, and he looked back, hoping to see another traveller or, even better, a car, but all he could make out was an shape undulating through the mist far behind him, so amorphous it could almost have been made of mist itself. Was that someone following him? And, if so, who?

Or what?

'Hello?' he shouted, but his voice was immediately swallowed up by the fog, leaving not even an echo behind it. And he couldn't see a thing now; if there had been someone behind him, they weren't there any more. Not as far as he could tell, anyway - it was hard to judge distances in this pea-souper. But wait! There was that faint scraping again. Vic forced himself to breathe more evenly. Seriously spooked, he tried to walk faster, but the sand was clinging to the soles of his shoes, and every step took an immense effort. His legs were aching, his heart beating fit to burst. Was that the sea he could hear, or the sound of muffled laughter? He didn't like this, didn't like it at all. Fuck the countryside! Or the seaside, or whatever this was. *Fuck it!* He hadn't signed up for this. He liked cities, where even when it was foggy you could see lights, and buildings, and cars, and people. Here it was just one big void.

The ground was getting softer, sucking his feet ever more deeply into the morass. His socks were full of mud and grit. The sand was swallowing his shoes like marshmallow and before he knew what was happening, he was up to his ankles in it, slowly but steadily sinking.

What the fuck?

Vic had read about quicksand in adventure stories as a boy, but this was the first time he'd encountered it in real life, and it was even more terrifying than he'd imagined. He had to get out of here! He tried to retrace his steps, but too late. Now he was up to his knees in liquid cement. The more he tried to struggle free of the sucking embrace, the more avidly it clung to his legs. Now he was really frightened. It couldn't end like this, could it? Buried in a bog in the middle of nowhere? No-one would ever know what had happened to him, and no-one would care. Diane? She wouldn't give a shit. Someone would eventually find his car, perhaps, but there wouldn't even be footsteps to them to follow.

'Is there anybody there?' he shouted, failing to keep the panic out of his voice, but sensing it didn't matter anyway, because there would be no-one there to hear his muffled death cries, as wet sand poured into his gullet and choked him.

But wait. Was that his imagination, or was it the shape he'd glimpsed earlier, flitting through the fog?

This was no time to be discreet.

'Help!' he yelled. 'Help! I'm sinking!'

He fixed his gaze on the outline, and prayed, but as the shape became more solid, icy fingers of doubt clutched at his consciousness. What *was* that? Was it even human? He squirmed desperately, unsure as to whether it was the deliquescent soil or the approaching figure that frightened him the more. But now the quicksand was up to his waist, so he had little choice.

'Help!'

The outline came into focus, and emerged from the fog, taking on the shape of a woman as it came.

It was Noreen Duval.

Despite the absence of wind, her black raincoat was billowing around her. She was wearing impossibly high heels which oddly enough, didn't seem to be sinking into the sand as she approached. When she had Vic within her sights she paused, coolly appraised the situation, and lit a cigarette.

What the fuck? Vic was agitated and embarrassed. Now the sand was up his shoulders, and he was having difficulty keeping his arms clear. And Noreen didn't seem to care two hoots.

'Get me the fuck out of here!' he shouted.

She blew a plume of lazy smoke out through her nostrils, making her face blend with the fog, and said, 'I like to see a man go down.'

Vic spluttered with indignation. 'I'll be going down for good if you don't fetch someone. For Chrissake, get help!'

'Keep your hair on,' said Noreen. Cigarette clamped between her lips, she stepped forward, grasped one of his arms and hauled him out easily of the quagmire, depositing him like a broken sparrow on more solid ground.

As he lay on his back, panting, Noreen leant over him, smiled, and held out her packet.

'Cigarette?'

*****

He was soaked to the bone, dripping with slime and shivering as convulsively as a lab rat wired up to an electric circuit. Both his shoes were missing, and he couldn't even remember what had happened to his bag.

He limped along the beach, leaning heavily against Noreen. She supported him easily, a rock in an ocean of shifting tides, seeming to glide over the surface of the wet sand.

Whatever gift she had, Vic wished he could share it. Every movement was an ordeal for him; with each footstep he could feel the last reserves of strength seeping out through his soles, leaving him an empty husk, propped up solely by the woman walking effortlessly at his side. And there seemed to be no end to the walking; he had no idea where they were going. Somewhere, a long way to their left, he could hear surf breaking, but all he could see was flat grey sand, and fog.

Noreen smelled like a hippy chick he'd once dated. Patchouli oil, that was what she'd worn. But Noreen's scent was darker and more mysterious and intoxicating. She was the sort of woman who went straight to your head, that much was clear.

At last, through drooping eyelids, he made out a dark shape up ahead. His spirits, already floundering near rock bottom, plummeted even further as he saw the unmistakeable outline of The Half Man emerging from the fog.

Vic's shoulders slumped in defeat.

'Fuck me, no. I'm not going back there. No way.'

'Not a lot of choice in this neck of woods, darling. You need to get out of these wet clothes. We don't want you catching your death. Not yet, anyway.'

'Who's we?' asked Vic.

Noreen tickled him under the chin. 'Also, you need a shave.'

*****

Twenty minutes later, Vic's wet clothes were steaming in front of the fire. The air was giddy with smoke, not of all of it coming from the fireplace. Perfumed grey coils unfurled vertically from a small thicket of incense sticks, while the mantelpiece and hearth were jammed with enough flickering tea lights to illuminate a small city.

Noreen's room was only slightly larger than Vic's, but the open fire made all the difference, and she had customised her environment with an array of exotic knick-knacks, silks and velvets and peacock feathers, so that it looked more like a courtesan's salon than a cheap bedroom over a bar. Her window, which had evidently escaped damage from the bomb blast, was swathed in filmy mousseline. The bedside lamp was draped with a crimson shawl, casting a rosy glow over the room.

The other notable difference between this room and Vic's was the prodigious quantity of baggage stacked up at the end of the bed. Vic had brought just one bag with him (and now, thanks to the quicksand, he didn't even have that any more) whereas Noreen had sailed in with a flotilla of stylishly battered leather suitcases, all of them plastered with retro luggage labels. Vic had only vaguely heard of some of the places she'd visited - hotels, airports or quaysides in Abyssinia, Tanganyika, Constantinople, Nyasaland, Tonkin, Cochin-China, Siam, Mogador... He'd never been awfully good at geography in school, but he knew enough to realise Noreen was at least as well travelled as Mrs. Saxby. These chicks were making him feel very unworldly.

Right now, though, Noreen was doing things that banished all thought of travelling from his head.

He was sitting naked on a wooden chair, steadying his nerves with regular nips from a bottle of

113

scotch as Noreen tickled his neck with Thin Tony's cut-throat razor. She was still wearing her billowing black coat, but now it was obvious there had never been anything underneath it. She rocked gently back and forth, buttocks rolling lightly against his thighs, legs hooked around his waist, trapping him in an erotic vice. Vic was torn between arousal and a discomfiting awareness that this beautiful stranger in the throes of mounting ecstasy was pressing sharp steel against his Adam's Apple.

Wiping a strip of lather from his chin with her sleeve, she leant back and ran a gold talon along Vic's tattoo, her eyes gleaming.

'So pretty,' she purred. 'Reminds me of my mother.'

'You mother had ink?'

'My mother was a snake! They drove her out of Ireland!'

Vic laughed weakly, though if this was supposed to be a joke he didn't find it very funny.

'French said you're not to be trusted,' he said.

Now it was Noreen's turn to laugh. Her whole body quivered with mirth. Vic winced, praying the razor wouldn't slip and slice into his carotid artery.

She stopped laughing and said, 'He's right. You shouldn't trust me. But don't trust him either. Always was a huckster of the blackest hue.'

'How would you know? You've barely spoken to him.'

'Oh, Mordecai and I go way back.'

Vic narrowed his eyes. This whole situation was getting odder by the minute, but it was difficult to think straight while his manhood was being rhythmically massaged by the rippling muscled sheath in which it was comfortably embedded. The best he could muster was, 'You don't seem the type to mix with coppers.'

Noreen cocked her head. 'Ever met a copper with a name like Mordecai?'

Vic tried to arrange his confused thoughts into some sort of order, but what with the smoke and the sex and the perfume, it was impossible.

'If he's not a copper, what is he?'

Noreen chuckled throatily. 'Honey, you wouldn't believe me if I told you.'

Vic said, 'Try me.'

Noreen rocked forward again, placed her mouth right up against his ear, and whispered, 'You're more of a man than he'll ever be.'

The flattering import of her words, together with the delectable tickling of her lips against his earlobe, tipped him over the edge. He began to pant and moan. Noreen rolled her eyes. She'd expected him to have more staying power. But it was not to be. She would just have to finish herself off manually.

Later, as they reclined on the bed, swathed in thick mink blankets and smoking her cigarettes, Vic remembered where he was and what had been happening, and tried to shake off the contented lethargy that was threatening to overwhelm him.

'That bloke, Griff. I know you said he was your dealer, but was he your boyfriend as well?'

Noreen smiled mysteriously. 'I guess you could say we were fuck buddies.'

'I'm sorry. It was a horrible way to die.'

Noreen shrugged. 'He's been through worse.'

Vic sat up. 'What could be worse than having your head cut off?'

'He's resilient. Goes with the territory.'

'*Was*. You mean he *was* resilient.'

'That's what I said.'

Vic persisted. 'But you two had sex?'

Noreen looked at him, a semi-smile hovering on her lips. 'Why, Mr. Pearce! Don't tell me you're jealous.'

Vic was indeed jealous, but had no intention of admitting it. He was also perplexed. For someone who less than twenty-four hours earlier had seen her lover decapitated before her very eyes, Noreen seemed remarkably sanguine. That unruffled attitude had surely to be concealing some kind of deep-seated trauma.

'How did you two meet, anyway?'

Noreen frowned, trying to remember. 'Midnight gig in Marrakesh, I think. You know he was a musician? Quite a talented one too. Everything from bass guitar to Peruvian nose flute, plus a couple of instruments your language doesn't have names for.'

'What I don't understand,' said Vic, 'is why you two bohos were hanging out with someone like Dr. Ridley. He seems so... straight.'

Noreen let out a peel of laughter. 'Straight? *Ridley?* That son of a bitch is as bent as they come.'

Vic was surprised. 'I hadn't pegged him as gay.'

'Gay? Lord, no. That would be *way* too normal.'

Vic hesitated before asking, 'You had sex with him too?'

She laughed again. 'You think one cha-cha gives you the right to cross-examine me about my sexual history? Not that I give a fuck. But I can never fathom you people and your funny little ways. I guess that's what turns me on.'

'It does?' Vic savoured a small thrill of satisfaction before adding suspiciously, 'What do you mean, *you people*?'

'Englishmen are so funny.' Noreen lit another cigarette. 'But no, Ridley's not my type, and never will be. He's a bastard.'

'You seemed quite chummy last night.'

Noreen gazed at him, as though weighing up whether to say more. 'Let's just say he tricked me once, and now I owe him. No getting round it, but as soon as I've returned the favour I can move on.'

'He's got something on you?'

'It's complicated.'

'And French, how do you know him?'

'Everyone knows French.'

'*I* don't,' said Vic.

'You do, you know. You just don't remember.'

Vic had a sudden flashback to French's face. Yes, now she'd mentioned it, the Inspector *had* seemed oddly familiar, though Vic couldn't for the life of him work out why, or how, or where they might have met before. He would surely have remembered a cop like that. You had to keep an eye on the fancy ones.

'What's he looking for? Is Ridley looking for the same thing?'

Noreen blew smoke in his face. 'Now then, I've already said too much. I wouldn't want to frighten you away.'

'Mrs. Saxby said I was in danger. Should I be worried?'

Noreen absent-mindedly began to caress his leg with her foot. There were silver rings on some of her toes, which made the caress all the more stimulating. The golden anklet gleamed.

'I've half a mind to nick your boyfriend's car and get out of here, said Vic.

'You wouldn't get far. They'd come after you.'

'Oh yeah? How? The Merc's a write-off.'

Noreen was looking at him almost sympathetically. 'You really don't understand what you're up against, do you, baby. Let's just say that as long as you still have arms and legs, you're in with a chance. An outside one, maybe, but a chance all the same. But if they caught you trying to make a break for it, they would have to make sure you couldn't run away again. Or crawl away, come to that.'

Vic couldn't tell if this was a threat or a warning. He opened his mouth to cross-examine her further, but before he could say anything, their post-coital glow was ripped asunder by an almighty ruckus from somewhere below: an outbreak of stampeding, and slamming, and indistinct yelling, followed by clattering and banging and more slamming, all of it coming nearer.

Before Vic had time to get up and put his clothes back on, there was a rude hammering at Noreen's door.

'Noreen! Get out here right now!'

Ridley.

'Her master's voice,' sighed Noreen. She got up and slipped a red velvet dress over her naked form.

More hammering, and Ridley yelled again.

'Noreen! Are you there? Brian Curtis has escaped!'

CHAPTER 8: WHERE THE SAMPHIRE GROWS

Vic's suit hung off him in crumpled folds, like skin from a Sharpei's neck, and yet the cheap fabric still clung to him in clammy patches wherever the slow toasting by Noreen's fire had failed to dispel the dampness. He was going to catch pneumonia on this damned trip, he thought miserably. *You wait, Turlingham you bastard.* All thoughts of fleeing the country had vanished from his head. He didn't yet know how he was going to get his revenge on Little Jimmy, but as soon as he got out of this shithole he would devote his every waking hour to the task. Always supposing Fat Tony and his companions didn't get to take him on one of their infamous jaunts to the Essex saltmarshes first.

It didn't help that his feet were bare, and the stone flags beneath his toes were as chilly as a witch's tit. He made a mental note to ask the Rocks if they had any spare shoes lying around. From the open doorway he squinted down into the dark cellar, parts of which now lay under several inches of water. Rock was splashing up and down between the wine racks, shining his torch into every nook and cranny, as though Brian Curtis had somehow managed to shrink himself down to the size of a bottle.

The only thing testifying to the missing prisoner's forced sojourn in the cellar was a pile of ratty blankets lying abandoned on a stone slab, some crumbs of toast on an empty tray, and two empty bottles. Curtis had clearly been availing himself of the refreshments on hand.

Inspector French was also down there, though he'd managed to keep his shoes dry and now seemed more interested in checking out the wine than in searching for the missing man. He extracted a bottle, dusted off the label with his hand and let out a whistle.

'Fifty-four! Fucking awful year.'

'We're wasting our time,' said Mr. Rock. 'He's not down here.'

'Well, duh,' Vic said at the top of the steps. 'I could have told you that from here.'

Hearing his voice, French looked up from the bottle, spotted Vic, and grinned.

*****

Mrs. Rock dunked a dirty glass in the sink and wiped it dry. Noreen was perched on a high stool on the other side of the bar, filing her nails. Ridley was examining the cellar door.

Vic laced up the old work shoes Mrs. Rock had dug out for him. They were too big, and one of the uppers was peeling away from the sole, but they were better than nothing, so he wasn't complaining.

When his feet were properly shod he allowed Kitty to snuggle up to him. He glanced over at Noreen, and was a little disappointed that it didn't seem to bother her. He was not displeased at Kitty's proximity, but uncomfortably aware that he hadn't had time to take a shower, leaving him smelling of swamp and sex. It didn't seem to be putting her off, though. Indeed, she was gazing at him imploringly with her big blue eyes.

'There's a killer on the loose,' she said, placing her hand on Vic's thigh. His eyes widened in surprise. He wondered if she'd done it accidentally. Maybe she thought it was his arm.

'I'm so scared,' she said.

'I bet you are,' said Noreen, turning her hand this way to judge which of her fingernails needed filing next. 'Poor pussycat.'

Vic permitted himself a small smile. Maybe she was a little jealous after all.

Ridley straightened up. 'Lock's intact. Nothing wrong with the bolts.'

'So how did he get out?' asked Vic.

'Obviously someone opened the door,' said Ridley.

'Who in hell would do that?'

French emerged at last from the cellar, Mr. Rock tagging obsequiously behind him, and immediately started ordering people around.

'OK. I want you, you and you to search the upstairs rooms,' he said, pointing at Kitty, Noreen and Ridley. 'You take a look outside,' he said to Mr. Rock. 'Nice to see you, Vic, good to have you back. I trust your meeting with the widow Saxby was productive?'

Everyone except Noreen turned to stare at Vic.

'You went to Saxby Hall?' said Mr. Rock. 'Without telling us?'

'Well now, Mr. Pearce,' said Ridley. 'Did the widow say anything of interest?'

Vic squirmed with embarrassment, as though he'd been caught skipping off school. 'Not really. Old

121

biddy was in her cups, ranting fit to bust. Can't blame her, what with her husband only just laid in the ground, and all. Her dogs were out of control.'

He decided not to mention Thin Tony.

'And what was she ranting about?' asked French.

'Do tell,' said Kitty, laying her head against Vic's arm.

Vic cast his mind back, trying to come up with something that wouldn't make him seem too much of a pipsqueak. 'Wittering about French cuisine, I think. I don't speak the lingo, but she mentioned Crème Brûlée...'

'Crème Brûlée?' said French. 'Are you sure?'

'And Châteauneuf-du-Pape, something like that.'

'Châteauneuf-du-Pape?' echoed Ridley. 'You talked about *wine?*'

They were all ears.

'Not really,' said Vic. 'Château... Châteauneuf-du-Pape... No, Crème Brûlée... Châteauneuf-du-Pape brûlé...'

'Brûlé...' said French. 'Brûlé...' His eyes suddenly opened wide, and then almost immediately narrowed into glittering slits. He turned to face Vic with an unnaturally wide smile. 'Ah yes, my kind of cuisine. They certainly know how to stuff a goose in La Dordogne.'

'She wasn't making a lot of sense,' said Vic, thinking to himself that the Inspector wasn't making much sense either.

But French kept smiling until it was quite unnerving. 'You can help me check the rest of the ground floor, Mr. Pearce. This idiot Curtis is a wild card. I want him taken off the board before he does any more damage.'

'What do you mean by *taken off the board*?' asked Vic.

'Locked up again. What else?'

'I won't feel safe unless I stay close to Vic,' pouted Kitty.

French glared at her. 'You'll do as I say, Miss Bridges. From now on, I myself shall be keeping a watchful eye on Mr. Pearce.'

'Oh, so I'm a suspect now,' said Vic.

'We wouldn't want you wandering off again,' said French.

'You told me to go!' said Vic.

'We'd hate to lose you in this fog,' said Ridley.

'Glad everyone's so concerned about my welfare,' said Vic, feeling as though he were back behind the bike sheds, with Charlie and the Micklin twins ganging up against him. It would be scuffed knees and bloody noses all round before you knew it.

French clapped his hands impatiently. 'Enough of this persiflage. Let's get on with it! Let's find Brian Curtis before he decapitates anyone else!'

*****

There was nowhere in Ridley's room for Brian Curtis to hide, but Kitty took the opportunity to search it thoroughly anyway. She flicked through Ridley's books, felt around between the crisply folded piles of underwear, checked beneath the mattress and shuffled through the folders on the dressing-table, pausing occasionally to speed-read the contents.

The doctor's effects were ranged with a tidiness bordering on the maniacal, so she took care to leave things exactly as she found them.

Finally, when she'd searched the luggage and papers, she knelt in front of the doctor's bag. It was locked, but she pulled a pin from her hair, inserted it into the lock, and gave it a wicked little twist. The mechanism sprung open with a click.

The bag was full of glass jars. Kitty extracted one and held it up to the light.

When she saw what was floating inside it, she giggled in childish delight.

*****

Brian Curtis was nowhere to be found in Kitty's room either, but Noreen and Ridley didn't let that deter them as they rifled though the contents of her matching monogrammed luggage, showing not the slightest inclination to leave things as they found them. Expensive garments went flying around the room in a whirl of costly colour and fabric, like Jay Gatsby's shirts.

Ridley almost passed over the neat stack of books on Kitty's bedside table, but something about them caught his attention. He looked more closely: the authors were Jackie Collins, Sidney Sheldon, Guy Debord, and Søren Kierkegaard.

*****

Vic opened the cupboard and checked behind the mops and buckets.

'You won't find him in there,' said Mrs. Rock.

'Probably on his way back to London,' said Vic. 'I know I would be.'

'Only if he's got a boat,' said Mrs. Rock.

'Ah yes,' said Vic, remembering the stream that had turned into a raging torrent. 'You know the bridge is down?'

'The bridge is always down,' said Mrs. Rock.

'It wasn't when I arrived,' said Vic.

'I was speaking metaphorically,' said Mrs. Rock.

While Vic was trying to work out what she meant by that, he heard French's voice coming from the taproom.

'In here, Mr. Pearce.'

Mrs. Rock tilted her head. 'Better do as he says.'

She returned to her favourite position behind the bar and started wiping glasses again. With a sigh of resignation, Vic obeyed the summons.

In the taproom, French was standing over the table, looking down at the bloodstained sheet covering Griff's corpse. He jerked his head at Vic and asked, 'What's wrong with this picture?'

Vic stared at the shape on the table for a few moments before gingerly lifting a corner of the sheet.

The colour drained from his face.

'Bloody hell,' he said.

French nodded. 'Looks as though Brian Curtis isn't the only thing missing.'

*****

Outside The Half Man, the wind whipped itself into a fresh frenzy, rattling the doors and howling down the chimneys once again. The search had been completed, but Brian Curtis was still on the loose.

Everyone convened in the bar to eat sandwiches.

It was already dark outside, but still too early to go to bed. After supper, Kitty and French started a game of billiards, each of them lining up and executing impossibly brilliant shots in which the click-clacking balls appeared to defy the laws of physics. Vic, who fancied himself a useful billiards player, had at first considered joining in, but when he saw what they were capable of he thought better of it. If his own youth had been misspent, he could only surmise that Kitty and French must have earned Master's Degrees at Bar Billiards University. As Kitty's latest punt skipped over three white balls and clicked gently against the red one, nudging it into the pocket, he shook his head. He just wasn't in their league.

Noreen sat at the upright piano, picking out random snatches of melody on the keyboard.

'Why would Curtis steal the head?' asked Kitty, as her latest pot ricocheted off a side cushion and wove in and out of the pegs like a squirrel running for cover.

'How do we know it was Curtis who took it?' said Vic.

'Who else could it have been?'

Ridley was playing an elaborate game of Solitaire on one of the tables. Judging by the way he kept glancing at his watch, he was playing against the clock. Vic stole a look at the cards as he wandered past and saw it was a foreign pack, covered with odd geometric symbols rather than the suits he was familiar with.

Vic wandered on to where Mr. Rock was propped up against the bar, on which he'd laid out all the antique firearms from the walls. Intermittently tippling from a large glass of whisky, he was loading the weapons with ammunition from cobwebbed boxes brought up from the cellar.

'If he tries anything tonight, we'll be ready for him.'

Vic looked dubiously at the firearms, all of them rusty and looking as though they hadn't been fired since the 19th century.

'Be careful with those things,' he said. 'Probably blow up in your face if you pulled the trigger. When did you last clean them?'

'Couple of weeks ago,' said Mr. Rock. 'Part of my job to keep this place in working order.'

The lights flickered and went out.

'Oh yes?' said Vic.

'Just a power cut,' said Mr. Rock.

French clapped his hands together in glee. 'I love power cuts!'

Mrs. Rock rounded up a number of candles of varying lengths which she jammed into the tops of empty bottles, then stationed tea lights on every available surface around the bar. They were undoubtedly a fire hazard, but with the flickering light and the glow from the open hearth, the place looked almost charming.

But evidently not to Ridley, who clucked with annoyance.

'For God's sake, man. Don't you have a backup generator?'

'Happens all the time,' said Rock. 'Won't last long.'

'I think it's romantic,' said Kitty, sidling up to Vic again.

Something had been niggling at the back of Vic's brain, but only now did he work out what it was.

'What about Sergeant Wheeler? Shouldn't he be back by now? Hope he didn't get lost in the fog.'

'No need to worry about Wheeler,' said French. 'Local lad. Knows these parts like the back of his hand.'

Noreen, bored by the conversation, was still picking out chords on the keyboard. As the talk petered out, she began to sing in a husky mezzo-soprano, her face and cleavage looking even more bewitching than usual thanks to the tea lights on top of the piano.

> *Lost I was, and hungry too*
> *The eastern mire was bleak*
> *The wind it chilled me to the bone*
> *And I was growing weak*
>
> *When then I spied a lovely witch*
> *Stewing supper o'er her fire*
> *O witch, I said, give me to eat*
> *And I will be your squire*

Vic thought the tune sounded familiar, as though it were something he might once have heard on *Top of the Pops*. But no matter how hard he tried, he couldn't remember the name of the song, or the singer.

French and Kitty seemed to find it familiar too, nodding along and tapping their feet. Mr. and Mrs. Rock kept their distance, as though they felt joining in would undermine their roles as innkeepers, and Ridley didn't even look up from his Solitaire. But French chipped in with the next verse, his voice a pure tenor that thrilled the ears.

And so to eat she gave me eels
Sautéed in butter in a pan
And I grew hale again and vowed
Fore'er to be her man

Noreen, still tickling the ivories with the casual expertise of a practised lounge-bar pianist, looked up at French and smiled conspiratorially at him.

Vic looked from one to the other, aghast.

'How can you people sing at a time like this?'

Noreen redirected her smile at him. 'No time like the present, Vic. Sing while the iron's hot.'

Not to be outdone, Kitty launched into the next verse with her clear ringing soprano:

The witch she took my hand and said
O I will be your bride
But if you do me wrong, beware!
You'll wish that you had died

And then, despite himself, Vic found himself singing too, though he had no idea how he knew the words. The lyrics must have embedded themselves in his brain at some point during his drug-addled teenage years. Or was he simply making the words up as he went along? Hard to say. But heck, everyone else was singing; he might as well join in.

So I thanked the lovely witch
And took her home to wed
And for a while our lives were bliss
Both in and out of bed

And then they were all singing in unison: Noreen, Kitty, French and Vic, who continued to come out with the lyrics, though he still couldn't remember how he knew them.

Now he listened, though, he wasn't sure he liked them much.

But then my eye began to stray
And I forgot my witchy wife
You are but half a man she cried
As she took up her knife

I saved your life and gave you eels
And you vowed you would be true
But now those vows have turned to dust
I'll cleave your flesh in two

And I will drink your blood like wine
And your bones will decompose
In the marshlands of the east
Where the samphire grows

'Whoah,' said Vic, who didn't care at all for the way the song had ended.

'Relax, Mr. Pearce,' said French. 'It's just a song.'

'Ridiculous,' said Ridley as he slipped his cards back into their case and got his feet. 'I'm going to have an early night.'

French grinned at him. 'Never did like people having fun, did you, Doctor?'

'May I remind you this is a serious business,' said Ridley. 'A great many lives are at stake.'

'Singing and dancing are against the doctor's religion,' said Noreen.

Ridley gave her a sharp look.

In response, she repeated the last verse of the song, smiling provocatively at the doctor.

> *And I will drink your blood like wine*
> *And your bones will decompose*
> *In the marshes of the east*
> *Where the samphire grows*

'What the hell *is* that song?' asked Vic. 'And how come I know the words?'

'Old English folk song,' said Noreen. 'Your mother probably sang it to you when you were a baby.'

'Not *my* mother,' said Vic, thinking of Sally Shoesmith of Worthing, who had run off with a plumber and left little Victor Ignatius in the care of his father, a post office clerk and keen amateur gardener who had forced his infant son to eat worms.

Ridley lost patience. 'Enough of this nonsense.' He grabbed the musket and the nearest candle before heading for the stairs, where he turned back to address the room.

'I'd advise you all to arm yourself. And don't forget to lock your doors again.'

CHAPTER 9: GREEN SMOKE

Still crooning to himself, Vic tried to open the door to his room, a relatively simple task complicated not only by his having to juggle the flintlock pistol and lit candle, but also by the fact that he was pickled.

> *In the marshlands of the east*
> *Where the samphire grows...*

Talk about an earworm. The song had slithered into his brain and was now chasing its own tail around in there. He couldn't get rid of the bloody thing. But he finally managed to unlock the door and wrestle his way inside. He placed the bottle with the candle on the bedside table before locking himself in, just as the doc had advised.

Then a gleam popped into his eye, like a shiny piece of fruit into the window of a one-armed bandit. Brian Curtis might pose a danger to the others, but not to him; the dweeb had approached him as an ally, not an adversary. He had nothing to fear. Unless, of course Curtis really was a psychopath. But even if that were the case, he was still a puny specimen. Vic reckoned he could take him easily in a fair fight. Or an unfair one, come to that.

So why not take advantage of the situation? Why not offer his services as a bodyguard, say, to a damsel in distress? What did he have to lose?

He reopened the door. The landing was spookily lit by storm lanterns that cast eerie shapes on the walls, but - buoyed by the whisky coursing through his system and the comforting heft of the pistol in his fist - Vic padded along the corridor to the last door on the left, took a deep breath, and rapped softly on it.

'Noreen,' he whispered as loudly as he dared. 'It's me, Vic.' And waited, feeling himself grow pleasantly tumescent at the memory of her straddling his lap, razor in hand.

There was no reply, but Vic thought he heard something moving inside the room. He pressed his ear to the door, and listened intently.

Two voices. One of them Noreen's.

The other was deeper. A man's voice.

He jerked away from the door as though it had stung him.

She had a man in there.

Vic couldn't place the voice, but whoever he was, he was making her laugh. The bitch was *laughing*.

He was taken aback by the intensity of the pain surging up inside him. He felt like kicking himself. She'd led him on and, like a mug, he'd fallen for her game. Served him right for being so soft. He should have known better than to trust a woman. They were all the same, cockteasers and ball-breakers, always messing with his head and taking advantage of his generous nature and ever-ready manhood.

Trying to downplay his despondency, he shuffled back to his room. He locked himself in again, sat down on the bed, and brooded.

'Slut,' he said, and felt slightly better. Converting the hurt into anger made it easier to bear. He was about to upgrade the insult to 'cunt' when a hand shot out from under the bed and grabbed his ankle.

Vic leapt to his feet, a shriek of horror rising to his lips. He managed to clamp his hand over his mouth before most of it escaped, not so much from discretion as a humiliating realisation that the sound was shaping up to be more high-pitched than was fitting for a tough guy such as himself. But a noise emerged nonetheless, and it wasn't pretty.

Brian Curtis crawled out from under the bed and smiled weakly up at him.

'Keep it down,' he said in a conversational tone. 'We don't want the others to know I'm here.'

Vic groped for the flintlock and aimed it at his visitor's head, mortified to see his hand was wobbling like a jelly. Christ, the nerd had given him a fright.

'You keep away from me.'

Curtis scrambled to his feet. He was rumpled and unshaven, covered in dried blood and dust. There was a crazed glint in his eye.

Jesus, thought Vic, *he really is insane.*

'You've got nothing to fear from me, Vic. I wouldn't hurt a fly.'

Vic laughed nervously. 'Maybe not a fly, mate, but I've seen what you do to *people*. And I'll use this if I have to.' He brandished the pistol. 'This isn't the first time I've held a gun to someone's head.'

'I don't suppose it is,' said Curtis. 'But while I was in that cellar I had plenty of time to think, and I'm not concerned for my own safety, Vic. It's yours I'm worried about.'

Vic shook his head in disbelief. 'Why is everyone so bloody worried about me all of a sudden?'

'Because you're special, Vic. Or hadn't you realised?'

He placed a hand on Vic's arm. Unable to tell whether the gesture was intended as a threat or a come-on, Vic backed away, still training the flintlock at Curtis's head. 'Bollocks to that. How did you get out of the cellar?'

'Someone opened the door,' said Curtis. 'Don't ask me who; I have no idea. But that's not important. What matters is this...'

The energy seemed to drain out of him, and he sat down heavily on the bed. 'You may think it's pure chance that your employer sent you up here, Vic. But it's not.'

'Of course it's not. I was banging his bird, and he wanted to remind me who was boss. But what's Turlingham got to do with it?'

'He wants what all of them want. Even if he's not sure what it is.'

'Enough of these fucking riddles! Who the hell *are* these people, and how do they all know each other? I don't trust any of them further than I could throw them, and I sure as hell don't trust *you*.'

'But you have to trust me, Vic. I'm your only hope. Only I can save you.'

Vic spluttered in indignation. The very notion of this nerd presuming he could watch out for a member of the Lewisham Contras struck him as farcical. It was like getting a Chihuahua to guard your Rottweiler. But he limited his retort to, 'Why don't I find that reassuring?'

'I've been keeping an eye on them for years,' said Curtis. 'And they're all after the same thing. No, I don't know what it is, but I do know it will bestow unimaginable power on its possessor. And you're the key, Vic. They need you to help them unlock it, and I daresay that doesn't mean giving you tea and biscuits. Which is why you've got to get out of here before midnight. You're dead meat if you don't.'

'So everyone keeps saying,' said Vic. 'But easier said than done. My motor's stuck in the mud, and we're stranded here, in case you hadn't noticed.'

All the same, his thoughts kept drifting back to the Alfa Romeo parked outside. Shouldn't be too difficult to hotwire. By the time everyone else woke up he'd have a head start. He was still drunk as a skunk, but it wasn't as though there would be a lot of traffic on the roads at this hour. The broken bridge? There *had* to be a way around it...

In any case, it was a plan. But he had no intention of sharing it with this maniac.

'It's the equinox *and* the Full Moon *and* Saturn enters Scorpio *and* Mercury is in retrograde,' said Curtis.

Vic sneered. 'Spare me the horoscopes, mate.'

'And Burvis-Tappa is only two billion miles from Neptune, the closest it's been to Earth in five hundred years!' Curtis was almost weeping with emotion. 'Whatever they want to happen *must* happen tonight!'

'Not if I can help it,' said Vic.

Curtis chewed his lip. 'It's not just about you. The fate of humanity is hanging in the balance. A battle between Good and Evil, and it's happening right here at The Half Man, Vic. Whoever comes out on top will reign unchallenged for another half millennium. And if we're not careful...'

Vic lost patience with his babbling. 'You're fucking loco, you know that? You cut someone's head off!'

'Mea culpa,' said Curtis. 'I thought Griff was the dangerous one, but I was wrong. The Big Cheese is still at large. I think you know who I'm talking about.'

Vic rose to the bait. 'Inspector French!'

Curtis nodded. 'The Inspector. I realised my mistake as soon as I heard his voice. Except...'

'He's not a real copper, I know.'

'We have to kill him,' Curtis said matter-of-factly. 'We have to kill them all. We can't leave a single one of them standing. But I can't do it on my own; I'll need your help.'

'You've got to be fucking kidding.'

'Wish I was,' said Curtis.

Vic decided to bluff. He didn't give a toss about the Inspector, but he had no intention of helping Curtis massacre Noreen and Kitty. Or Mr. and Mrs. Rock and Dr. Ridley, come to that. But he needed to play for time, get the little man to trust him. Maybe he could be lured back down to the cellar and locked in there again.

'OK, but first tell me this, you nutjob - why did you steal the fucking head?'

Curtis looked indignant, as though he'd been accused of sexual deviancy. 'You think I...?' For a while his lips moved, but no sound emerged. He seemed to be debating with his inner voice. *Or voices,* Vic thought.

Finally making up his mind, Curtis got up and unlocked the door.

'Come with me, Vic. I'll show you what happened to the head. Maybe then you'll take me seriously.'

Vic followed him out into the corridor, but cautiously. Was this a trap? He didn't dare drop his guard, or his gun. He didn't *think* Curtis was in league with any of the others, but he was learning not to take things at face value. Nobody here was what they appeared to be. He vaguely recalled French telling him something like that... and French himself was a liar.

Curtis crept along the passageway to Noreen's door and placed his ear against it, just as Vic had done a few minutes earlier. He beckoned.

Reluctantly, Vic approached.

Ears pressed against the door, they could both hear Noreen on the other side. She was still conversing with her mystery guest. Or was it the murmur of canoodling lovers? Vic felt his temper rise again. He'd thought she had genuinely liked him, yet here she was, throwing herself at anything in trousers. Well, see if he cared. He felt like barging in and catch her red-handed with this other bloke, whoever he was. Just let her try and explain!

Curtis was watching him carefully.

'Tell me, Vic, do you believe in the paranormal?'

'Fuck off,' said Vic.

'Then I suggest you brace yourself. Your entire belief system is about to undergo a radical restructuring.'

Taking a deep breath, Curtis tested the doorknob... and found Noreen hadn't bothered to lock herself in.

'Welcome to my world,' said Curtis. He pushed the door open and stepped across the threshold.

It was some time before Vic's mind was able to get to grips with what his eyes were showing him. Once again, Noreen's room was lit by the flickering flames of a hundred tea lights, transforming it into a magical cavern out of the Arabian Nights. Noreen was sitting on the edge of the bed, looking darker and more alluring than ever, her profile, as usual, wreathed in cigarette smoke. She was too engrossed in conversation to notice the visitors. Or maybe she *had* noticed, but just didn't care.

'You'll never guess who turned up then!' said Noreen.

'Go on, darling, give us a clue.'

Only now did Vic recognise the male voice, and his blood ran cold. No wonder it had sounded familiar. Identifying it had taken him longer than it should have done, but since none of what he was seeing or hearing made sense, he had a legitimate excuse.

The mystery man was Griff.

Or, rather, Griff's *head*, which Noreen was cradling in her lap. She was talking to it, and Griff was holding up his end of the conversation without apparent difficulty, chattering away, even though his neck ended in a gory stump.

'Monte Carlo, 1959?' said Noreen. 'Babies' brains, still warm from the cranium? Underwear fashioned from lambs' eyelids?'

'*No!*' said Griff's head.

'*Yes!*' said Noreen. 'Calling himself French.'

Vic was appalled. Never in his life had he seen or heard anything like this. Not even when Turlingham had lost his temper and sliced one of Portly George's foot soldiers right down the middle. Not even when Lenny Mangola had gone bananas with a shotgun in the The Royal Duck.

This was a whole new order of mayhem.

'Told you!' said Curtis, so proud at having forced Vic to confront the truth that the exclamation came out more loudly than intended.

Like plants responding to photosynthesis, Noreen and Griff's head swivelled slowly towards the sound.

'Well, look who's here,' said Noreen, face hardening into a Medusa-like mask. She was no longer the temptress who had forced herself on an all-too-willing Vic. Now she looked meaner, and more dangerous.

'Well fuck me up the bum with a dead monkey's dick if it ain't The Decapitator,' said Griff's head. 'Knocked off any good blocks lately?'

Noreen lifted the head from her lap and placed it gently on her bedside table, from where it continued to survey the room. Turning back to Curtis, she said, 'Didn't your mother ever teach you to knock, little man?'

Curtis was terrified, but resolute. 'Game's up, Miss Duval. Vic knows everything.'

'No I don't,' said Vic.

'Don't waste my time, you pathetic little squid,' said Noreen. 'What conceivable threat do you think you could you ever pose to someone like me?'

In answer, Curtis reached into his capacious poacher's pocket and drew out a small mallet and a sharpened stake. 'Never underestimate a pathetic little squid in an anorak!'

Noreen glared at him contemptuously. 'What do think I am, a fucking vampire?' She took an extra deep drag of her cigarette and held it in for a moment before expelling an abnormally large murky green cloud directly into Curtis's face. He stumbled back, coughing.

Noreen began to laugh. And laugh.

At first, the laughter sounded normal, but gradually it changed pitch, gaining in sharpness and volume, until the room was filled with an ear-piercing, nerve-shredding banshee shriek. It was so painful Vic tried to block his ears, though the attempt was hampered by the flintlock in his hand.

Curtis summoned his courage and sprang forward, jabbing uselessly with his stake. Noreen swatted him aside as if he were a gnat.

'Do him, Noreen,' said Griff's head.

The candles flared up and went out, all at once, all one hundred of them.

Behind Vic, the door slammed shut with a force that propelled him forward.

The green smoke spread until it filled the room, making Vic and Curtis cough and splutter. At the heart of the cloud, Noreen shimmered with an eerie sepulchral glow. Her long black hair took on a life of its own, tresses flying out around her head as if caught by an invisible wind. Her eyes flashed darker than the obsidian pits of hell.

The banshee shriek subsided into a hiss.

Vic tried to back towards the door, but found his feet rooted to the spot. He couldn't move.

Curtis looked as though he was beginning to regret his rash action. Despite his decades of diligent research, he hadn't foreseen anything quite like this.

Noreen's arms melted into the side of her body. The folds of her skirt grew longer and leaner. Her skin was tinged with green. She grew taller, and more slender, until she was looming over the cowering Curtis, peering down into his upturned face.

Vic was unable to pinpoint the exact moment of the metamorphosis. It could have been a trick of the light. All he knew was that Noreen had somehow changed into a giant green snake, with glittering eyes and a flickering forked tongue and shimmering scales.

Her long tail whipped out and wrapped itself around Curtis's legs, bringing him crashing to his knees. The little man screeched, his eyes bulging in terror. In a movement faster than lighting, the head of the snake swooped down and bit his face off. What was left of him collapsed on to the carpet in a bloody mess, and lay there twitching.

Vic's fear gave way to pity and disgust, and then the appalled realisation that he was next. But before he could uproot his feet and make a run for it, Noreen had shrunk back down into human form. There was still something shimmery about her, particularly around the edges, but she was almost back to her old self.

She lit another cigarette and licked the blood off her lips. 'Boy, I needed that.'

Griff's eyes were fixed on Vic. 'What about the other one?'

'He'll keep,' said Noreen.

Her eyes widened in surprise as she felt the ornate muzzle of the ancient flintlock jammed up against her temple.

'You're wrong,' said Vic, who still wasn't sure how he'd managed to get the drop on her. Evidently his fighting instincts had taken over while his mind was still paralysed. 'I go off very quickly.'

Noreen recovered her sang-froid. 'Tell me something I don't already know.'

'You shouldn't have killed the nerd,' said Vic, looking sorrowfully at Curtis's faceless corpse, which had finally stopped twitching. 'I'm beginning to think he wasn't mad at all. He had *your* number.'

Noreen laughed scornfully. 'Baby, everyone's got *my* number.'

'You can't touch me,' said Vic, trying to sound braver than he felt. 'You need me for something. '

'Maybe the others do,' said Noreen. 'But not me. I like you, Vic, I really do. Maybe in another life we could have had fun together, but I don't *need* you for anything. In fact, if I were to kill you now it would be doing the world a favour.'

Vic's gun hand wavered. 'Then why did you save me from the quicksand?'

'Quicksand!' exclaimed Griff. 'You never mentioned quicksand!'

Vic addressed the head. 'Did she also tell you we made love, right here in this room?'

'Made love?' Griff frowned, as though this were a technical term he didn't understand.

'We fucked,' prompted Noreen.

'Oh yeah,' Griff said with a toothy grin. 'Oh yeah, she told me all about *that*. Fact is, we had a proper laugh about it.'

Vic felt stung. It wasn't his fault he'd ejaculated prematurely. 'You women,' he muttered.

'What do you reckon, Psycho Boy?' Noreen asked the head. 'Fuck, marry or kill?'

Griff's head said, 'I reckon you should go where your fancy takes you, princess. Let the rest of them go whistle.'

'Exactly what I was thinking,' said Noreen.

Ignoring the pistol, she leant towards Vic and kissed him full on the lips. He flailed around blindly, feeling her long tongue working its way into his mouth, and her arms entwining him in a smothering embrace. It was just like his nightmare! He squirmed in vain, panic rising in his chest as he realised he had no way of releasing himself from what was obviously shaping up to be a death grip. He struggled for air. There was a bitter taste in his mouth. His vision turned red.

Noreen was sucking the life out of him.

Worse, he could feel himself *enjoying* it. The blood rushed from his head to his groin like a herd of stampeding stallions. This was the way his world was going to end, he realised, with one big head-splitting, mind-blowing, asphyxiating orgasm. He could feel it building up inside him now, a solfatara emitting jets of steam, preparing to blow him apart, like the island of Krakatoa...

Every muscle in his body begin to spasm, and, more by accident than design, his finger stiffened on the trigger of the ancient flintlock, which exploded with a flash and a bang. There was a sudden surge of oxygen into his numbed brain and the infernal pressure vanished from his chest. The barrel of the pistol had bloomed into a blackened daisy wheel, miraculously leaving his fingers intact. He staggered back, ears ringing, red and green slime dripping from his hands and face.

To his astonishment, Noreen seemed unscathed. Only when she turned her head towards him did he see that a large segment of it was missing. On what was left of her face, there was an expression of surprise, and disappointment.

'You idiot,' she said. 'You went off early again.'

And with that, she crumpled to the floor.

CHAPTER 10: THE NIGHTWATCHMAN

The door flew open and hit the wall with a crash. A shrill scream split the air.

Vic thought, *Oh bollocks, what now?*

The ruined pistol still smoking in his hand, he turned to face the music.

Kitty and Mr. Rock were standing open-mouthed in the doorway. French was peering over their shoulders with keen interest.

Vic tried to summon a reassuring smile. But he was splattered in gore, and dripping with green slime, and on the floor behind him lay two corpses with ruined heads in spreading pools of blood. It occurred to him this might not look good.

Mr. Rock, tweed jacket over his pyjamas, was pointing a shotgun. His other arm was draped protectively around the shoulders of the distraught Kitty, whose baby doll nightdress made her look indecently young, casting the innkeeper in the role of stern-faced paedophile.

French was as immaculately dressed as ever, as though he hadn't even bothered to go to bed.

'My God!' gasped Kitty. 'You killed them!'

French gave a wry smile. 'Looks like we caught you green-handed, Mr. Pearce.'

'I can explain,' said Vic, and proceeded to do so, though if he'd had a moment to consider his predicament, he would probably have thought twice about babbling the words that popped into his head. 'Noreen turned into a snake and killed Brian Curtis... We found her talking to Griff's head and it was talking back to her...'

The three people in the doorway turned in unison to stare at Griff's head, still sitting on the bedside table where Noreen had left it. The head's eyes were filmy. It looked very, very dead.

'It *was* talking,' said Vic. 'I swear!'

'Of course it was, dear boy,' said a soothing voice from the doorway. Ridley had just arrived on the scene with his doctor's bag. Like French, he was fully dressed, as though he'd never had any intention of going to bed.

Vic stared in bewilderment at the inanimate head sitting on the bedside table like a macabre novelty lamp that no-one wanted to switch on. Had it all been a nightmare, after all? Maybe he'd been sleepwalking. But in that case, how had the...

The head winked at him.

Vic jabbed his finger accusingly. 'It winked at me!'

But by the time the four people in the doorway turned back to look at it, the head had already resumed its lifeless expression.

'Of course it did,' said Ridley.

'It was you all along!' said Kitty. 'You stole the head, and then when Miss Duval and Brian Curtis found out, you murdered them!'

Vic sighed. 'Why the fuck would I steal the head?'

'Because you're insane!' cried Kitty.

'I'm beginning to think I'm the only sane one in this madhouse,' said Vic. But he sensed he was fighting a losing battle. They'd been looking for a scapegoat, and now they'd found one.

French stepped in front of Kitty and Mr. Rock. 'I'm afraid it's your turn to be locked in the cellar, Mr. Pearce. Are you going to come quietly, or do we have to manhandle you?'

'Now wait,' said Vic. 'I haven't done anything! I demand to see my lawyer.' He didn't actually have a lawyer, but he'd heard the line many times on TV cop shows.

French raised an eyebrow. 'Haven't done anything? Now that's not quite true, is it, Mr. Pearce? By fortunate coincidence, I ran your name through the database yesterday...'

From an inside pocket with all the spatial properties of Doctor Who's Tardis, he drew out a long coil of continuous form paper covered in print. 'Let's see... Breaking and entering, several counts. Damage to property. Offence against public decency. Possession of unlicensed firearm. Forgery. Stealing a dog. Obstruction of justice. Extortion. Embezzlement. Armed robbery. First degree murder...'

Mr. Rock whistled. 'Well, that escalated quickly.'

'I never stole a dog!' Vic was beside himself with outrage. 'And I never killed anyone! And even if I did, it was self-defence!'

French sprung forward and pinned him in an armlock so tight it cut off circulation to his hands. 'Are you sure about that, Mr. Pearce? Come on, let's get this miscreant downstairs.'

He paused to look around Noreen's room in disgust, nostrils flaring, before nodding at Mr. Rock. 'Clear this mess up, will you. And for heaven's sake open the window. Stinks like a cheap brothel in here.'

Mr. Rock curled his lip, clearly not happy at being addressed like a lackey on his home turf. He pointedly turned his back on the 'mess', and stalked out of the room. Vic's spirits rose at this sign of mild rebellion, only to be dashed again as he found himself being frogmarched into the passageway.

'You're making a mistake,' he said. 'Let me call Turlingham. He can explain...' He squirmed like a fish, trying to free his arms.

French bent to whisper in his ear. 'Haven't you guessed yet? Your boss set you up.'

'Fuck you!' said Vic, trying to nut the Inspector, who dodged the blow without releasing his captive's arms. Vic wished Noreen were still alive; she would have known what to do. She might have been trying to crush the life out of him, but he already missed her. She hadn't been like the rest of them.

Course she hadn't been like the rest of them, he thought. He'd seen her turn into a giant fucking snake. What about the others? Were they *all* going to turn into giant snakes? He resumed his struggling with renewed vigour.

'Perhaps a mild sedative,' said Ridley, producing a syringe.

The doctor seemed more rational than the others. Vic tried to appeal to his common sense. 'You don't understand, Dr. Ridley. Brian Curtis was trying to warn me.' He jerked his head back at French. 'This man is not a cop.'

'Don't be silly,' said Kitty. 'He arrived in a police car.'

'He eats babies' brains!' said Vic.

French chuckled indulgently. 'And very delicious they were too. Now let's put you in a safe place.'

He began to steer Vic towards the stairs. But before they'd taken more than a few steps, a harsh voice behind them stopped French in his tracks.

'You're right, Mr. Pearce. He's not a cop.'

Vic was forced to stop too. He twisted his neck to look round at the speaker. Mr. Rock. His shotgun was levelled at French's back.

'I don't know about babies' brains,' said Rock, 'but I could tell you a thing or two about *Detective Inspector French*, as he calls himself.'

French didn't look round, but loosened his grip on Vic, who stumbled aside, out of range of the shotgun, trying to massage the feeling back into his arms.

'You idiot,' said French, visibly annoyed as he finally turned to face the innkeeper. 'I told you you'd get paid in full.'

'And I'm beginning to think it isn't enough,' said Mr. Rock. 'Whatever you're looking for is worth more than that. A *lot* more.'

'For God's sake, Rock!' said Ridley. 'No need for unpleasantness. Put the gun down.'

With everyone's attention fixed on the angry innkeeper, Vic spotted an opening. There were four people now standing between him and the top of the stairs, but maybe he could dive into one of these rooms and lock the door. He was sure that, between them, they could break it down easily enough, but the delay would give him just enough time to knot some sheets together and...

He felt a hand descend on his shoulder. Ridley whispered in his ear, 'Stick with me, Mr. Pearce. I'll keep you safe.'

Vic hovered uncertainly. 'Why should I trust you?'

'Because he mustn't find what he's searching for.'

'And what *is* that?' asked Vic. 'Everyone keeps going on about it, but no-one will tell me what it *is*.'

Ridley shook his head. 'I'm as much in the dark as you. All I know is we can't allow Mordecai French to get his hands on it.'

Mr. Rock backed towards Ridley, talking over his shoulder. 'That's right Doctor. You have no idea what our so-called Inspector is capable of. He was the one who planted that bomb in the car. He killed his own man!'

'Don't be absurd,' said French.

'Why would he do that?' said Ridley.

'Why don't you ask him?' asked Mr. Rock. 'He's the one giving the orders around here. I'm just the nightwatchman.'

'Exactly,' said French, growing impatient. 'A low-order batsman, paid to play host, prepare the ground, and keep his fucking mouth shut. I don't have time for this.'

'You think I don't know what you are?' said Rock. 'Brian Curtis wasn't the only one who did his research.' He looked at the others. 'Did you know, for example, that our so-called *Inspector French* once had a...'

French cut him off. 'Oh fuck it. You're more trouble than you're worth.' Without even looking at

Kitty, he snapped his fingers and said, 'Take it away, Miss Bridges.'

A change came over Kitty. Vic tensed, hoping she wasn't going to turn into a snake, but she merely adjusted her attitude, which flipped in an instant from flighty debutante to girl on a mission. With preternatural poise, she started to trot away from them, towards the stairs, before turning back to face them. Pulling her shoulders back, she drew herself up to her full height, paused for a deep breath, and accelerated along the passageway, an Olympic gymnast sprinting towards the vaulting horse, feet skipping over the floor as lightly as a dancer in a Japanese anime.

Knowing what was coming, French calmly stepped out of her way. Ridley pulled Vic flat against the wall as Kitty shot past them like a bullet and launched herself feet first at Mr. Rock, striking him square in the chest. Something broke inside him with a sickening crack, and he screamed in pain. As the blow propelled him backwards through the air, his nerveless fingers tightened on the trigger, just as Vic's had done earlier, and the shotgun let fly with both barrels.

For a moment, Rock's shape was silhouetted against the picture window, like a cartoon character being punted into outer space. Then with another scream, he crashed backwards through the glass. He fell out of sight, but they all heard him hitting the ground. Vic ran to the broken window to look outside. A blast of freezing air hit him full in the face as he gazed down at the man splatted on the stone flags below, limbs twisted like smashed pretzels. Blood, black in the moonlight, began to pool beneath the shattered head.

Vic felt sick, but as he turned back towards the first floor passageway he was faced with an even more unnerving sight. Kitty Bridges was staggering around, staring down blankly at the crater in her stomach ringed by a spreading nebula of pockmarks. But there were no blood and guts - just a tangle of springs, cogs and gears spilling out through a jagged wreath of splinters. From inside her came a mechanical whirring noise.

'My God!' said Vic.

Ridley shook his head. 'I might have guessed.'

'Sorry baby,' said French, more disappointed than upset.

At the sound of French's voice, Kitty went haywire. She began to spin from wall to wall like an out-of-control top, arms and legs scything through the air like dangerous weapons.

'For Christ's sake, do something,' said Vic as one of her hands gouged a diagonal slice out of the wall.

French, already bored by the spectacle, turned away to light a cigarette. 'Bit of basic carpentry and she'll be good as new.'

Ridley ducked under one of the flailing arms and, in a deft movement, unclipped first one of Kitty's earrings, then the other. The whirring noise stopped and she sank to the floor.

Vic gaped in astonishment. 'What did you do?'

Ridley was studying the earrings with interest. He held one up to the light from a storm lantern, and shot French an admiring glance. 'Koneko Mark Five. *Wissenschaft durch Magie.*'

'What the fuck?' Vic looked from Kitty's shattered body to Ridley and back again. 'Shouldn't we call an ambulance?'

Ridley pulled a small pair of tweezers from his bag and began to peel back the surface of one of the earrings, exposing the miniscule workings of a precision instrument.

'Science through magic, Mr. Pearce. Our Miss Bridges here is made of wood.'

Vic stared at him uncomprehending, then lost it, stamping his foot like a kindergarten pupil throwing a tantrum because someone had nicked his favourite crayon.

'Will one of you please tell me what's going on? I just came up here to get one lousy signature and what do I find? Snake women, talking heads, robot society girls! Bloody Halloween, that's what! She's not a real woman, he's not a real copper. I suppose you're not a real doctor.'

'Of course I'm a real doctor!' huffed Ridley. 'I've saved hundreds of lives.'

'I don't believe you!' said Vic. 'I don't believe anything any more. This is not my idea of fun. All I want is to go home and put my feet up and watch telly. I'm a Crystal Palace supporter, for heaven's sake. Christ, I need a drink.'

French lifted his wrist and coolly checked his Omega Co-Axial Moonphase Chronograph before looking directly at Vic.

'I'll buy you a drink, Vic. Least I can do after unjustly accusing you of so many heinous crimes. Obviously someone set you up; probably that fatburger boss of yours. Let's talk it over downstairs, man to man.'

Vic turned to face him, eager for explanations.

French smiled, and walked towards him.

Ridley looked up from the earrings and frowned.

'Don't listen to him, Mr. Pearce. He's not...'

Too late. The last thing Vic saw was French's fist drawn back and then looming bigger and bigger as it came towards him, fast.

And then CRUNCH!

Everything went black.

CHAPTER 11: HELL

Vic's head was throbbing. He was having to breathe through his mouth because his nose was blocked. Obviously he was coming down with a cold. No wonder, after all that wading through the freezing mud.

It had to have been a dream. The sort of dream you had after a truckle of Double Gloucester washed down with several pints of filthy stout. The château was burning. It was also upside down, and so blurry it was though Vic's eyesight had been infiltrated by the coastal fog in which he had so recently got lost.

There was something coiled around the flaming ruins. Only when the image swam into focus was he able to identify it as a dragon. Or possibly a giant serpent. It made him think of Noreen Duval, and he shivered. Had that been another dream, or had he actually had sex with a snake woman? Would you classify that as bestiality? Or was sex with snake women called something else?

And what about Kitty Bridges? Not a snake, but some sort of sexbot. The thought both excited and revolted him. And the way Griff's head had carried on talking even after it had been separated from his body? None of this was possible, not in Vic's world, so logic dictated it *had* to have been a dream.

And yet here he was. Even if this wasn't a dream, he could tell the castle and the serpent, or dragon, or whatever it was, weren't real. They were part of an engraving which his slowly recovering senses told him

155

was part of the label on the dusty bottle of wine being dangled in front of him.

'1499,' said a voice smoother than a cream-based whisky liqueur, 'and I don't mean the price. A very special year.'

French. Only now did Vic recall the fucker had socked him in the face. Christ! He tried to feel his nose, to see if it was broken, but discovered to his chagrin that he couldn't move his hands. He craned his neck. He was lying on a stone slab, wrists and ankles bound with cord tied in fancy knots.

The Inspector loomed over Vic, face sleek and spiteful in the flickering candlelight. It was as though electric light bulbs had never been invented.

Whoever these wankers are, thought Vic, *they certainly like their fucking candles.*

He twisted his head and saw row upon row of wine racks stretching into shadow. He was in the cellar, that much was obvious. The water had receded, leaving the sloping stone floor waxy and damp, with only a few shallow puddles and a smell of mould to testify to the earlier flooding.

'Turks took Montenegro. Albrecht Dürer's Apocalypse. Leonardo Da Vinci's Last Supper. Lucrezia Borgia - oh my, she was a charmer. The Black Death. A grand time to be alive! Ah yes, I remember it well.' French was apparently in the grip of some kind of nostalgic reverie. Vic felt a surge of irritation.

'Didn't realise they even had bottles back then. Didn't they drink out of flagons, or sheep's bladders?'

French gave a start, as if part of the furniture had just gained sentience and started talking. 'Of course we had bottles! You think we were primitives? We were

156

more civilised than you philistines could ever be! But in any case I'm talking about the engraving, not the wine.'

'How old *are* you?' asked Vic, trying to stay calm even though he could feel his heart hammering like a piston. Best to try not to provoke this creep. Try and keep him talking.

'Do you know, I lost count,' said French. 'Never could get the hang of the Gregorian Calendar.' He smiled toothily, and for an instant his face took on such an ancient and malevolent cast that Vic wondered how he'd ever put his trust, however fleetingly, in such a creature.

'You're not a cop, are you.'

'And you, Mr. Pearce, are not the brightest bulb in the chandelier.'

'At least I don't go round pretending to be what I'm not.'

'You see in me only what you want to see,' French said equably. 'You know how the human eye perceives things upside down, but the brain automatically adjusts the image so it appears the right way up? One could say I'm part of a similar phenomenon.'

'So you're really upside down?' Vic was perplexed, all the more so because, from his supine position, French really did look the wrong way up.

French laughed nastily. 'In a manner of speaking.'

'Are you even human?'

'Now you're talking,' said French. 'As Aristotle once said, men are but fleshbags, useful only as shopping trolleys or sex toys, their sole function to help ease the higher mindfulness of gods into the light.'

'Aristotle?'

French smiled condescendingly. 'Centre forward for Inter Milan.'

Vic ground his teeth in annoyance. Did French think he was stupid? Oh yes, he reminded himself, that's *exactly* what he thought. But they'd all underestimated him, all of them, from the very beginning. Maybe he could use this to his advantage. His mind raced as he considered the limited options open to him. He'd been in situations tighter than this...

No, wait. He hadn't.

'Go to hell,' he said.

French had begun to pace up and down the cellar, declaiming like a demagogue, though still careful to step around the puddles.

'Hell? *Hell?* You know what hell is, Vic? *I* know what it is. I've done time there, more time than you could ever imagine. Hell is a place where you can't smoke, or drink, or fuck people up the bum, or do any of those other deliciously wicked things we enjoy so much. Jean-Paul Sartre was wrong! Hell isn't other people. In hell you're on your own, and when it all gets too much and you're gibbering with rage and boredom and frustration, all you want to do is bite your own head off, except that you haven't got a fucking head to start with, so tough titty. When you're ready to explode with the frigging tedium of it all, you can't even toss yourself off, choke the chipmunk, beat the meat, tickle your pickle, because you have nobody. I mean you have *no body*, not in hell. No mouth. No cock. No balls. No arse. No organs or orifices. Nowhere to stick your finger. You're marooned in a sort of bleeding metaphysical state of incorporeality. Do you know what that's like, Vic? It's *boring.* Hell is *boring.* I'm not going back there, not if I can help it. And this baby's going to give me another five hundred years of fun, fun, fun, till my daddy takes the T-bird away. Another five hundred years of *heaven*, that's what's in it for me.'

Vic stared blankly at him. 'Am I the only human being in this place?'

'Ooh no,' said French. 'Rock was one of your lot. So's the good doctor, even if he has been around longer than most. Got to admire the fellow's staying power. Fifteenth century alchemist, don't you know.'

French bent over him. He stank of expensive perfume, and something else. Vic couldn't understand why he hadn't noticed it before. French smelled like scorched earth.

'You, on the other hand, are a typical twentieth century idiot,' French went on. 'A man of very little brain. I would have preferred a better vintage, maybe even Ridley himself. But beggars can't be choosers. You'll do.'

'I'll do what?' asked Vic, trying again to raise his head.

French leant against the nearest wine rack and lit another unfiltered Boyard. 'All right, let's play Twenty Questions. What's the name of this establishment?'

Vic, feeling as though he were being tormented by a sadistic history teacher, strained to remember. 'The Half Man?'

French smiled. 'Unusual name for a hostelry, don't you think?'

'Makes a change from The King's Testicles.'

French leaned closer so he could blow smoke into Vic's face.

'What does a name like that suggest to you?'

Vic coughed and closed his streaming eyes. And found himself watching a series of rapid flashbacks projected on to the inside of his eyelids.

Thin Tony's razor bisecting a stuffed olive, exposing scarlet innards.

Curtis's cranial glaive sweeping through the air and slicing through Griff's neck, unleashing a gout of arterial blood.

Noreen's razor biting into Vic's jugular... No wait, that didn't happen. Or did it? Maybe he was already dead, and this was some kind of peculiarly irritating afterlife.

He opened his eyes again. French was still standing over him. But now the pseudo-cop's elegant fingers were wrapped around the handle of a small machete, of an ornate design Vic had never seen before.

French noticed his curiosity, and turned the weapon this way and that, so it caught the candlelight.

'Ancient Babylonian. Impeccable craftsmanship... Well, that goes without saying, seeing as it has outlived everyone who ever wielded it. Nearly everyone, that is.'

He ran his thumb along the edge of the blade, and licked the fine line of blood which welled up and almost immediately faded away, leaving the flesh unmarked.

A flicker of horrified comprehension tickled the inside of Vic's brain. Except he didn't comprehend anything, not really. All he knew was this was the tightest spot he'd ever been in, even tighter than when Strangler O'Rourke and Murray Bashman had cornered him in the car park of the The Three-Legged Horse and had only been interrupted in their administration of cricket bat justice by the fortuitous arrival of Barf Martin and his brothers.

But Barf Martin had been pushed off a platform at East Croydon into the path of the oncoming London to Brighton express three years ago. Rodney was rumoured to be propping up one of the bridges over the M4. And no-one had seen hide nor hair of Bill the Pill since he'd set out for Bolivia to sort out the botched deal with the La Paz cartel. There wouldn't be any brothers coming to the rescue this time.

French laid down the machete. 'I did promise you a drink. He picked up the dusty bottle again. 'Fancy some of this?'

Vic nodded miserably.

French grinned. 'Well, you can't have any. I need it to maintain my current lifestyle. I've become addicted to this fabulous body, these classy togs, this stylish cigarette habit. Not forgetting the rest of the drugs. And sex, lots of sex, all sorts of sex, I'm not fussy. In fact, once the deed is done I might celebrate with the bottom half of your corpse. No, Vic, this wine is all mine.'

He put down the bottle and ripped Vic's shirt open to expose the snake tattoo. Vic flinched as French ran his fingers over the blue and green scales etched into his torso. It felt like the antic scampering of poisonous spiders over his skin.

'As good as a dotted line! So helpful of Turlingham to prepare the ground. That was some weekend, huh?' He untucked his own shirt and lifted it an inch or two, exposing a glimpse of green and gold scales. 'Snap! I've got one too! Though of course mine's more of a fuzzy old antique.'

161

'You were there?' said Vic. He tried to think back, but his memory of the stag weekend was still like a bad dream, all cloudy impressions, and running, and screaming, and spurting arterial blood.

'Stag do and a half,' said French. He picked up the machete again and looked down at Vic with one eye closed, like a darts player preparing to unleash his missile. 'Normally this part would come later, but it doesn't make much difference, not if you're me, so let's get the fun stuff out of the way first. Sayonara, Mr. Pearce.'

Vic knew only too well what would come next. He turned his head so he wouldn't have to watch the blade swooping down towards him...

And saw Ridley peering down at him from the top of the steps, draped in a surgical gown and lugging two large leather holdalls.

'Ah, there you are,' said Ridley, setting one of the bags down.

'Help,' Vic said weakly. 'He's going to kill me.'

Ridley looked vexed. His voice echoed through the cellar. 'Did you really think you could get away with it, Mordecai? With me here?'

Still gripping the machete, French turned to look up at the doctor, and smiled superciliously. 'Sorry Magnus, not enough to go round this time. I'm signing up for another five hundred years, and there's not a fucking thing you can do to stop me.'

'Oh, but I think there is,' said Ridley. He made an elaborate pass with his free hand, like a bandleader, and muttered something beneath his breath.

The bonds melted from Vic's wrists and ankles, leaving him staring dazedly at his untethered limbs.

'For God's sake, man, *move!*' said Ridley.

Vic rolled sideways off the slab, just in time. The machete blade whistled down, missing his hip by inches, and embedded itself in the stone amid a small explosion of sparks. French tugged at the handle in annoyance.

'Should have know you'd rain on my parade,' he snarled.

'*Copacabana con capita!*' yelled Ridley. Reaching into his bag, he pulled out something the size and weight of a bowling ball, which he hurled down the steps. It bounced once or twice and rolled to a halt in front of French.

Griff's head.

'Come to me of your own free will, Mr. Pearce,' said Ridley. '*Now!*'

Vic didn't need any more prompting. He hurled himself towards the steps and, shirt flapping loose, began to scramble up them.

French started after him, only to stop with a yelp of surprise. Vic looked back and saw the Inspector furiously shaking his leg, trying to dislodge Griff's head, which had sunk its teeth into his foot and was clinging to it obstinately, like a pitbull.

'These are two thousand dollar shoes, you ape!'

Vic turned and took the rest of the steps as fast as he could.

'Thank goodness I got here in time,' said Ridley, ushering him into the bar, and bolting the cellar door behind them.

'Yeah, where *were* you? I was very nearly chopped salami there!'

'Preparing my arsenal,' said Ridley. 'You can't go up against a creature like French unarmed.'

There was a roar of outrage below them, and the door quivered on its hinges. Ridley turned to face it, his hands moving rapidly in a series of double-jointed configurations.

'Won't hold him for long,' he said. 'We need to get out of here.'

Vic ran to the front door and flung what was left of it open...

Only to stop on the threshold, his eyes opening wide.

'I thought Rock was dead.'

'He is,' Ridley said, joining him in the doorway.

'Then why is he standing right in front of us?'

Rock was indeed standing in front of them. The late innkeeper's head lolled from his neck at an unnatural angle, and there was a jagged piece of white bone sticking out of his thigh. His complexion was deathly pale and spattered with blood. Parts of his brain were visible through the ragged breaches in his smashed skull, and yet he was still somehow managing to stay upright. His lips curled back from the broken teeth as he said in a cracked voice, 'I told you, Mr. Pearce. It's one big dead spot around here.'

The walking corpse reached for Vic, who let out a whimper and hopped backwards into the bar.

Ridley carefully placed his one remaining bag on a table. 'For heaven's sake, Mordecai. Enough with the pranks already.'

'What's going on?' asked Vic.

'Game of chess,' said Ridley. 'Two grandmasters marshalling their pawns.'

'I'm not a fucking prawn,' said Vic.

Ridley sighed. 'You will be if I don't get you out of here.'

Mr. Rock lurched forward into the bar and tried to wrap his hands around Vic's throat. Ridley plucked the darts out of the dartboard, shouldering Vic aside, and flung them rapidly, one after the other, at the reanimated corpse, muttering as he did so. To Vic's addled ears, the incantation sounded something like *Bristoliamus huntinigen jokkiwilsingus.* But he could well have been mistaken.

The innkeeper stood there for a moment, dead eyeballs criss-crossing like prison searchlights as they tried in vain to focus on the three missiles embedded between his eyebrows.

'One hundred and eighty!' said Ridley, before finishing with another tongue-twisting incantation. Mr. Rock's damaged head swelled and burst apart like a ripe watermelon. His body toppled sideways, what remained of his brains sliding out of his skull in a disgusting compôte of scarlet and grey.

There was a mighty howl from the cellar, followed by a great deal of thumping and crashing, as though a drunken rock star were smashing up his hotel room.

Ridley retrieved his bag, grabbed a billiard cue and kicked Mr. Rock's remains out of the way as he stepped out into the night. Vic, whose only plan of action was to get as far away from the machete as possible, had little choice but to follow.

Outside, the wind was vicious in its inconsistency, changing direction every few seconds. The Half Man sign creaked ominously as it swung from its gallows. Vic's eyes fell on Griff's red Alfa Romeo.

There was no-one to stop him now! He sprinted towards it and vaulted into the driver's seat. Just like a TV cop! But progress stalled as he fumbled around beneath the dashboard, trying to find the wires that would get him out of there.

Like a judgement from the elder gods, Ridley's hand came down on his shoulder again. 'Leave it, Mr. Pearce. He won't need a car to outrun you.'

'What the fuck is this guy? A were-whippet?'

Ridley didn't smile. 'Worse. Much worse now we've made him angry. Our only chance now is to head for the sea. If there's one thing he hates, it's water.'

*****

As though it had been rigged with Semtex, the cellar door exploded outwards. French strolled through the wreckage into the bar. Without even bothering to take aim, he lobbed Griff's now inactive head into the space behind the bar, where it landed in the bin with a dull thump, like a rotten cauliflower.

He paused to stare at the remains of the front door, banging in the wind, though the faraway look in his eyes indicated he was focusing on something far beyond it. He tilted his head slightly, as if to savour the rhythm, before suddenly whirling round and setting out in the other direction, towards the stairs.

*****

The tide was out. Dark clouds scudded across an even darker sky, trying and failing to block the light of the bulbous moon casting silvery stripes across the sand like the glistening trails of a giant slug.

Ridley strode towards the constantly rumbling sea, visible only as a thin roiling line of white on the distant horizon. Vic toiled after him, envying the older man his energy and speed. Even burdened with his large leather bag and billiard cue, the doctor's pace never slackened. Vic was handicapped by the sand clinging like glue to the soles of his borrowed shoes, trying to suck them from his feet the way it had stolen the last pair.

Ridley glanced irritably over his shoulder. 'Get a move on, Mr. Pearce!'

Ten minutes later, and Vic was hopelessly out of breath. The sea didn't seem any closer. From the corner of his eye he spotted a small dark shape on the shoreline, and gratefully stumbled to a halt. 'Is that a... man out there?'

Ridley stopped and squinted into the distance.

At first the shape appeared to be a static black dot. Then they saw it was moving, gradually getting bigger as it approached. As it came closer, they realised it wasn't walking, but running full tilt towards them.

'That's a uniform,' said Ridley.

Vic heaved a sigh of relief. 'Sergeant Wheeler! He must have got through!'

He didn't get time to wonder why Wheeler would be returning to The Half Man on his own, because the cop was getting closer by the second. As he approached it became increasingly obvious there was something not quite right about him, but it wasn't until he was almost on top of them that Vic saw what it was. The sergeant's dark uniform was glistening with seaweed. His skin was covered in barnacles. Worst of all, his face was twisted into an expression of purest malice. He no longer looked anything like the friendly copper Vic had last seen vanishing into the gathering fog.

As Wheeler reached them, Vic's nostrils filled with the foulest stench he had ever smelled, but before he knew it the policeman was rushing past him... straight at Ridley. The running man knocked the doctor flat on his back and dropped to his knees on his chest, sending the air shooting out of his lungs. He wrapped his barnacled hands around Ridley's throat and began to squeeze. The doctor's arms and legs flailed uselessly. He made choking noises, eyes rolling back in his head.

Vic turned to looked longingly at the faint outline of the inn behind them, where the Alfa Romeo was parked. There was still time to make a run for it.

On the other hand, the doctor *had* saved his life. Vic's personal code of ethics was shaky at the best of times, but he prided himself on returning a favour. And so he turned back towards where Ridley was having the life throttled out of him and dealt the kneeling cop a robust kick to the head. It was a tactic that had always worked for him in Lewisham, and it worked for him here, even better than expected. As though Wheeler weighed nothing at all, he went hurtling sideways and landed with a soft squelch on his back. He lay like an upturned beetle, opening and closing his mouth.

Leaving Ridley to struggle to his feet, Vic stared down at the thing that had been Wheeler.

'Christ, man,' said Vic, not without pity. 'What happened?'

Wheeler's cracked lips moved, and sound came out. 'I drowned.'

Vic stared aghast at the skin caked in barnacles like the crusty pustules of a virulent plague. Wheeler's mouth opened, as if to say something else, and a crab scuttled out. The man's eyes stared out in stark terror, as though there might still be a remnant of something human behind the grotesque mask. But before he could make another sound, the disfigured face disintegrated into a mush, smashed into pulp by Ridley's heel. With an expression of intense disgust, the doctor continued to grind his foot into the sand, as though crushing every last vestige of life out of a cockroach.

Finally, the doctor turned his back on the corpse, loosening his collar to massage his bruised neck. 'Another of French's blasted pawns,' he wheezed. 'Or prawns, if you will.'

'What the hell *is* French?' asked Vic

'Babylonian prankster,' rasped Ridley, still rubbing his throat. 'Heaven help the human race if he drinks what's in that bottle.'

'You mean the wine?'

'Not wine,' said Ridley.

'What is it then?'

'Blood.'

*****

On the first floor landing of The Half Man, French was kneeling over Kitty's prostrate form. Next to him, on the floor, lay an open leather case containing an array of intricate tools, of the sort one might have associated with an artisan watchmaker, or possibly a dentist. A look of intense concentration on his face, he probed the gaping hole in the girl's abdomen, first with a delicate

169

pair of pliers, plucking and twisting, and then with a pencil-sized wand which emitted a luminous blue light as he soldered two wires together. There was a faint buzzing, followed by a satisfying click.

'There you are, my sweet. Good as new.'

Affectionately, he smoothed Kitty's hair back from her face, gazing deep into the bright staring blue of her lifeless eyes.

'Time to bring you back into play, my pretty.'

From his bottomless inside pocket he pulled out a pair of glittering earrings, not unlike the pair Ridley had removed earlier, and clipped them into place on her perfect lobes. He drew back to regard her critically for a moment before digging into his pocket again, this time drawing out a fine silver necklace. Tenderly, he fastened it around her neck, making sure not to get her hair caught in the clasp.

Then he got to his feet and twisted his fingers into an anatomically impossible shape, muttering an incantation under his breath.

Silence.

But then, from deep within the girl's abdomen, a faint clicking and whirring.

In an abrupt movement, Kitty sat upright, and began to turn her head from side to side, like an epileptic bird. Gradually the convulsive movements slowed until, finally, her eyes came to rest on French's, and her mouth split wide open in a beam of innocent delight.

'Mordecai!'

'Hello, my lovely.'

She frowned prettily. 'I was the most beautiful girl in the ballroom, and all the men wanted to waltz with me, and I held them so tightly and whirled them around so fast that their ribs cracked and they screamed in pain and their ears began to bleed. Was that a dream?'

French chuckled indulgently. 'In a manner of speaking, Miss Kitty Bonecracker. It was a long time ago. But how would you like to crack some more bones for me now?'

'Ooh yes please!' said Kitty.

CHAPTER 12: THE SANDS

Ridley had finally stopped walking. Vic leant forward with his hands on his knees, sucking in great draughts of sea air as he tried to recover from the exertion. He watched the doctor set his bag down on the sand, open it wide, and lift out a series of small glass jars filled with cloudy liquid. Within the swirling murk floated small slithery objects and unidentifiable animal parts. Vic kept watching, curious despite his revulsion. The doctor unscrewed the tops of the jars and then, with a pair of long silver tweezers, extracted the contents and planted them in the sand, each one a short distance from the next.

And all the while, he was muttering under his breath.

'What are you doing?' asked Vic.

'Elementary self-defence,' said Ridley.

'Yeah, like that's going to stop him,' said Vic, sceptically eyeing the nearest object: a bright blue eyeball. It swivelled in its sandy niche to eye him right back.

'Knowing what I know about our friend, it should hold him just long enough.'

'You've met him before?'

'You could say we share history,' said Ridley. 'Now let me finish or he'll be flaying the skin from our faces and feeding our tongues to his cats.'

He dug one last hole and planted a wriggling wormlike creature in it before straightening up. Walking backwards, wielding the billiard cue like a giant calligraphy brush, he began to trace an elaborate sequence of symbols in the sand. To the untrained eye, they might have been Arabic, Chinese or ancient Egyptian. But they were probably something even older.

Vic recovered his breath, more or less, and at last found himself able to stand up straight again. But fatigue was pressing down on him like a suitcase full of stones. He didn't want to be here, shivering on this godforsaken beach, being stalked by forces he couldn't begin to understand. He wanted to be back in Lewisham, necking Black Monk and chain-smoking and watching telly from his bed as Crystal Palace scored goal after goal after goal...

His head dropped forward so violently it jerked him awake, and he realised he'd nodded off on his feet.

Ridley was looking around with an air of satisfaction.

'Et voilà!' he said with a sweep of his hand. *'Cultivons notre jardin!'*

The words jingled a small bell in Vic's memory.

'That's what Mrs. Saxby said!'

'Did she now,' said Ridley, suddenly distracted. He'd caught sight of something in his tracings he didn't like the look of. Muttering like an absent-minded geometry teacher, he strode briskly over to the offending glyph and rubbed it out before starting all over again.

Vic felt the hairs on his arms stand on end. Something was happening. He shivered, though not from the cold. Green smoke coiled upward from the sand, only to be snatched off course by the antic wind.

The air filled with hissing, as though there had been a mass breakout from a reptile house at the zoo.

And all of sudden, Noreen Duval was there.

'Hello big boy,' she said to Vic. 'Miss me?' Despite the grievous injury to her head, she seemed to be walking and talking as normal. Or as normal as anyone could be who ought to have been dead.

Vic, now wide awake, spluttered in consternation. 'I killed you!'

'Takes more than a pop gun to put me out of action,' she said. 'Isn't that so, Doc?'

She stepped up to Vic and enveloped him in a warm embrace. It was tight, but not uncomfortably so, like the last one she'd given him. And even now, with the contents of her head smearing against his shoulder, he was finding her hard to resist.

'Get off me,' he mumbled, without conviction. 'I don't hobnob with birds who try to kill me.'

Noreen chuckled indulgently. 'Oh baby, did you really think I was trying to *kill* you? Time you learned the difference between sex and death. Close neighbours, but not compatible.'

Ridley made an impatient clucking sound. 'Come along now. We don't have time for shenanigans. French is preparing his endgame.'

'Always the party pooper,' said Noreen, peeling herself away from Vic with a sigh, leaving him puckering his lips against empty space.

'Need I remind you our arrangement has not yet been terminated,' said Ridley, frowning down at one of his symbols and making a minute adjustment to the angle of a stroke.

'You never *stop* reminding me.' With her one remaining eye she winked at Vic. 'Later, darling.'

Without warning, she was knocked sideways by a whirling automaton of action.

Vic had no idea how Kitty had managed to sneak up on them, but nothing surprised him any more. For all he knew she'd materialised out of the ether; these people were anything but normal, he knew that much. But the robot society girl he'd last seen lying on the floor with her guts a tangle of cogs and splinters was now hunkering down in attack mode, ready to rumble, baby doll nightdress hanging off her in tatters but her abdomen apparently good as new. She was smiling at Vic, but there was no warmth to it, there had never been any warmth there. But there was definitely a malicious gleam to her eyes that he hadn't noticed before, and a silver necklace that caught the moon's rays and spat them back again in piercing shards of light.

'Hello Vic,' she said, flexing her triceps. 'Don't worry, I'm not going to kill you. Just break your arms and legs so you can't run away.'

'Like hell,' said Vic, planting his feet apart. She wasn't so big; he reckoned he could take her, even though he generally made it a rule not to hit women. He lowered his head and was on the point of charging, fists at the ready, when he hesitated. He'd just remembered the noise Mr. Rock's ribs had made when she'd cracked them.

Kitty was hopping from one foot to the other, like an eager flyweight. Vic steeled himself for the onslaught, determined to put up a fight, at least. But to his relief, she turned her back to him and began to jog in the opposite direction. He felt a little prickle of pride. Running away! She'd probably realised he wasn't going to be a pushover, like Mr. Rock. Maybe she'd even got wind of some of his legendary exploits with the Contras.

The relief was short-lived. After twenty yards, Kitty turned back to face him, the lovely face marred by a cruel smile that promised nothing but pain, and he realised to his dismay she'd just been giving herself room to work up speed.

Ridley looked up from his symbols and saw Kitty lowering her head like a bull. Off to one side, Noreen had lit a cigarette and appeared to be sulking.

'For God's sake, Noreen,' said Ridley. 'Why do you think I brought you back? Do your thing!'

Noreen rolled her eyes. 'I don't need *you* to bring me back, Doc. I can come and go any time I please, remember? And I don't need one of your wretched blood rituals to do it. You and French, you're so fucking full of yourselves.'

'I am *nothing* like that reprobate,' snapped Ridley. 'And you know it.'

Noreen dropped her cigarette, stamping it out beneath one of her heels. 'Yeah, yeah.' She mimed masturbation with her hand.

'I *save* lives,' said Ridley.

'You've also taken a few,' said Noreen.

Vic felt desire welling up inside him once again. This dame was quite something. He liked the way she talked back at Ridley, even though the doctor clearly had some sort of hold over her. What on earth could it be? Money? Blackmail? Vic couldn't imagine. This chick was shameless. All she wanted was to get drunk and fuck and take drugs and talk to severed heads and turn into a snake goddess and bad things like that. She was his kind of woman, all right, even with half her head missing.

His reverie was rudely interrupted as Kitty let out a piercing battle cry and began to sprint back towards him, arms and legs pumping. He wavered like a goalie facing a penalty. Left or right? He needed to make his mind up quickly, because she was coming up fast.

Before he could reach a decision, Noreen threw herself at the running girl, knocked her off balance and wrapped her legs around the slender waist, velvet dress riding up to expose her stocking-tops.

Cat fight! Vic tried not to enjoy the spectacle, but the way the two women were rolling around on the sand, kicking their legs and squealing and tugging at each other's hair made it difficult not to get turned on. As the struggle rolled them further and further away, and with it the danger, he couldn't help feeling flattered. Two hot chicks, fighting over *him*. He decided he was rooting for Noreen; she might have tried to squeeze him to death, but at least the experience had given him a hard-on. Kitty, on the other hand, he wasn't so keen on. He saw nothing remotely erotic in getting his arms and legs broken.

Without looking up from his brushwork, Ridley said, 'Earrings, Noreen.'

'Enchanted bling!' said Noreen. 'Of course!' Her legs still wrapped around Kitty's waist, she threw back her head and laughed gaily as she plucked first one, then the other earring from her opponent's earlobes. Kitty went limp, a puzzled look on her face.

Noreen scrambled to her feet and looked at the earrings in her palm with interest, before sliding them into her cleavage.

But Kitty wasn't finished. With a noise like a zip being pulled, she shook her head so violently the features blurred. Then she was leaping to her feet and repeatedly punching the squelchy side of Noreen's head. Bits of blood and brains went flying as Noreen tumbled on to her back, long golden fingernails scrabbling at the sand.

'Sod this for a game of soldiers,' she said, hauling herself to her feet again.

Kitty adjusted the weight to her back leg, gearing up for a kickboxing roundhouse. As she turned sideways her silver necklace caught the moonlight again. Now Vic was certain she hadn't been wearing it earlier.

'Noreen!' he shouted. 'The necklace!'

Noreen dodged the flying kick and lashed out at Kitty's face, leaving vivid striations down her cheek, like lovers' initials carved in oak. She snatched at the necklace, but Kitty was bounding around again, indefatigable. With a sharp hiss and burst of green smoke, Noreen tried to transform into her snake shape but Kitty wrapped her in a wrestling hold and lifted her into the air.

Vic was no longer enthralled. Now he realised he was watching a fight to the death, and that he was going to be in deep shit if Kitty came out on top. The struggle was taking the two women away from him, further along the beach. Maybe there was still time for him to make a break for it... But he sensed that, even with a head start, he wouldn't have the energy to outrun the robo-girl.

'Come on, Noreen!' he muttered. '*Come on!*'

But something had changed. The women's movements were less fluid, more effortful. Vic edged towards them, trying to see what was going on. As he got nearer he saw what was happening. Kitty was up to her ankles in wet sand, weighed down by Noreen.

'Quicksand!' yelled Vic, and began to run towards them.

Ridley glanced up from his symbol-tracing. 'No, Mr. Pearce! You need to stay here.'

Vic ignored him.

Kitty stared down curiously at her disappearing legs before the reality of her situation impressed itself on her, and she began to kick her way free. But the effort loosened her grip on Noreen, who finally succeeded in ripping away the necklace as she fell.

The instant the chain parted company with her neck, Kitty shut down. Her dead weight sank like a heavy statue, the semi-liquid sand rapidly consuming hips, torso and head, until all that remained were a few large bubbles bursting on the surface.

'Christ,' said Vic.

But his erstwhile rescuer was in trouble too, already up to her armpits in the sand. Vic threw himself flat and stretched out an arm. 'Grab my hand.'

'Let her go, Mr. Pearce,' called Ridley, still engrossed in his writing.

Noreen ignored Vic's helping hand, and used her own to blow him a kiss, just before the sand claimed her arms.

'You must be thirsty, Vic. But there's plenty to drink here. Grab it while you can. Remember that.'

'No, wait,' he said.

'Bottoms up!' She tipped her face back just before the quagmire closed over her head. The last Vic saw of her was a half-smile in the moonlight. And then she was gone, leaving nothing but a small green swirl on the surface of the sand.

She'd been right. Vic *was* thirsty, spitting feathers in fact, but she was wrong about there being plenty to drink. Nothing but miles and miles of sand and seawater. He stared at the small green swirl until even that had dissolved, and felt the ground beneath him shift treacherously. The quicksand was trying to suck him down too. He scrabbled backwards out of the danger zone. Only when he'd drawn level with one of Ridley's glyphs did he feel safe enough to stand up again.

'She's gone,' he said, moving back towards Ridley.

'Oh, I doubt that,' said the doctor. He put the finishing touch to another of his elaborate symbols and straightened up to face him. 'There!'

As if on cue, French emerged from the empty air, as if stepping out of an invisible door, and placed a proprietorial hand on Vic's shoulder. In his other hand was the ancient Babylonian machete.

'Check,' he said. 'Your move, doctor.'

'I've already made my move,' Ridley said with a thin-lipped smile.

He cast the billiard cue aside and spread his arms, palms upward, as though calling down rain from the heavens.

Vic looked around. Only now did he see that, all this time, the doctor had been tracing a large circle in the sand. A gigantic fucking circle, its circumference marked by small wriggling creatures, dead animal parts and ancient alchemical symbols.

All three men were standing inside it.

Vic had no intention of letting French hack at him again. He kicked the Inspector's ankle as hard as he could, wriggled free of the hand and began to run... only to trip over the squirming hindquarters of a reptile planted in the ground. He went sprawling face down.

From somewhere just behind him came malicious laughter. He rolled over and sat up to face it. French was sauntering towards him, moonlight glinting off the raised machete.

'Let's cut through all this red tape, shall we? Let's do the show right here.'

With nowhere left to run, Vic sighed and closed his eyes and waited for the coup de grâce.

It didn't come. He reopened his eyes just in time to see the machete drop from the Inspector's numbed grasp. The demon clutched his wrist, and tried to step closer to Vic. But he couldn't. He raised his arms and tried again, but something was stopping him. His palms were flattened against the air, like a mime artist encountering an invisible wall.

'What's the matter, Mordecai? Can't break the circle?'

French turned back to face Ridley. 'You think this pathetic bag of tricks is going to stop me?'

'Under normal circumstances, it wouldn't,' said Ridley. 'Certainly not if we were in the Sahara, or the Gobi, or any of those other arid wastelands you love so much. But look where we are!'

For the first time French looked, *really* looked. And so did Vic.

'Not keen on getting your feet wet, are you, Mordecai?'

French turned to face the sea, and saw the tide racing in. For the first time since Vic had met him, he looked discomfited.

Ridley was unable to suppress a leer of triumph. 'And it's North Sea salt. Your favourite.'

French bounded across to the other side of the circle, only to find himself once again hemmed in by Ridley's invisible force field. Realising he'd been tricked, he threw back his head and let out a nerve-shattering roar of fury. Vic quailed, covering his ears to try and block out the sound.

Livid with rage, French whirled round and launched himself straight at Ridley's throat. The doctor calmly stepped backwards out of the circle.

'I'll get you for this!' screamed French, all traces of human conviviality gone.

Ridley chuckled. 'Not for another half-millennium, you won't.'

French went mad. He tore around the circle, ricocheting off the perimeter like a wildcat with a firework tied to its tail, screaming and hissing and scratching at the air. When it was clear that brute force wasn't going to help, he whipped round to claw at Vic like a junkie reaching for his fix. Vic shrank back in horror at the sight of those formerly handsome features twisted into a terrifying mask. Or perhaps he was simply seeing French's real face at last.

At that moment, the first wave of the incoming tide dissolved the seaward segment of the circle. French saw it, and realised there was only one course of action left to him.

'See you in hell!' he screamed at Ridley, and spun round on the spot like a dervish, faster and faster, almost faster than the eye could see, before breaking free of the sandstorm he'd whipped up and racing towards the ocean, gathering even more speed and howling as he went, long coat flapping behind him like the trailing wings of a giant bat. As the two thousand dollar shoes came into contact with the seawater, there was a blue flash and the sound of celestial fabric ripped asunder. The coat was on fire, or perhaps it was French himself who was burning. As he splashed across the shallow water, the flames devoured his body until he was blazing like a Roman Candle, running towards the ocean, spitting curses and sparks.

Vic put a hand up to shield his eyes. There was one last dazzling flash, as though all the lightning in the heavens had converged on the exact same spot. French was there, and then, in the blink of an eye, he was gone, leaving nothing but a patch of churning, boiling water and the smell of sulphur.

Vic rubbed his eyes.

'Where did he go?'

'He went home,' said Ridley, and patted Vic's shoulder. 'Looks like it's just you and me now, Mr. Pearce.'

'Thank God,' said Vic. He'd had enough of this lark. He was exhausted. 'I really do need a drink.'

He continued to stare at the spot where he'd last seen French, blinking rapidly to try and dispel the after-image scorched into his retinas. So he didn't notice Ridley bending down to pick up the ancient Babylonian machete. Nor did he sense the doctor walking up behind him and calmly bringing the blunt end of the handle down on the back of his head.

All he knew was sudden darkness.

Again.

CHAPTER 13: THE HALF MAN

To wake up and find yourself tied to a stone slab in the cellar might be described as unfortunate. But even Vic had to concede that to wake up a second time and find yourself tied to the very same slab smacked of carelessness.

Jesus H. Christ. Why hadn't he made a run for it when he'd had the chance? Why had he let his fucking sense of honour get in the way?

Oh yes, because he'd trusted Ridley. The man was a doctor, with a sober, distinguished demeanour. Vic had always been a sucker for well-spoken authoritative figures who looked as though they knew what they were doing. And Ridley had known what he was doing all right.

So now here he was: shivering on the slab, barefoot and stripped to the waist, helpless as a lump of meat waiting to be carved. He glared with loathing at Ridley's back. The doctor had removed his surgical gown. His shirtsleeves were rolled up, and his shoulders were heaving. Was he crying? Of course not. What did *he* have to cry about? *He* wasn't the one who'd been bashed over the head and tied to a fucking stone slab. Twice in one fucking night!

Despite his predicament, Vic found himself laughing. He wasn't scared any more. He was *beyond* being scared. Maybe he *ought* to be scared, but now he was just pissed off. No, worse than pissed off. He was hopping mad. Or would have been, if only his feet had been free to hop.

'Glad to hear you in such good spirits,' said Ridley.

'What the fuck are you doing?' said Vic.

Ridley turned round. He was grappling with a corkscrew that was firmly embedded in the neck of a bottle. The same bottle French had shown Vic earlier: the one with the burning castle and a dragon, or possibly a giant snake, on the label.

'If only Mordecai hadn't been so keen to sell his allies down the river in 1848, there might have been been enough to go round, but this is the last remaining dose. Hidden in plain sight, though I don't suppose we could have got anywhere near it if old Saxby hadn't popped his clogs in time. Just in time, as it turned out.' Ridley checked his Rolex. 'In exactly twenty minutes and fifteen seconds, it will lose its potency. Which would be a tragic waste.'

'And none of you wankers had anything to do with the clog-popping, of course.'

'As a matter of fact, we didn't. Nature took its course, and Saxby *was* exceedingly old. But if it makes you feel better, I'm simply reclaiming what was already mine. This prize was stolen from me by the widow Saxby's father. That mountebank got what he deserved, but I made the mistake of thinking he would be working alone. Had I known he would be so tasteless as to drag his *daughter* into the affair, I would have adjusted my security measures accordingly.'

'So what happens when you drink it?' asked Vic.

Ridley permitted himself a grin. The effect was quite ghastly. Once again, Vic couldn't understand why he hadn't looked at any of these people more closely. The man was clearly a shark.

'I'll have another five hundred years,' said Ridley.

Vic rolled his eyes. He'd thought Ridley the sane one, but he was just as mad as all the others.

'Oh, don't look like that,' said Ridley, misinterpreting his captive's reaction. 'I'm a neurosurgeon, Vic, and an excellent one at that. Have you any idea how many lives I've saved over the years? Admittedly the tools were a little primitive in bygone days, and I've had my failures like everyone else, but my contribution has been broadly beneficial, and I have no doubt my good deeds will continue to be of service to mankind for another five hundred years.'

'Well drink it then, and stop boring me death,' said Vic.

The doctor tugged at the corkscrew again, but the bottle seemed loath to cede its contents too easily.

'Your entire sordid little life has been nothing but a prelude to this moment, Vic, or didn't you realise? No, I don't suppose you did. You never were very smart. But you should count yourself privileged to be a part of this, to be contributing, albeit in a humble way, to something far greater and more momentous than your primitive intellect could even begin to grasp.'

He set the bottle down next to half a dozen empty ones on an empty shelf, untucked his shirt and lifted it. To Vic's amazement, around the doctor's waist wound a snake much like his own, except the scales were red and gold instead of blue and green.

'French had one like that,' said Vic.

'That's because we're members of an exclusive club. There are certain conditions that need to be filled, certain... blood rituals, shall we say. I think you've performed at least one of those in your career, Vic, though admittedly not without help.'

'The stag party,' said Vic. 'What did you make me do?'

'Oh, you didn't need much persuading. You're a natural.'

'No I'm not,' said Vic. 'Those drinks were spiked.'

'Not the drinks,' said Ridley. 'The drugs now, they were another matter. And you're a very suggestible man, Mr. Pearce. A half-cocked pistol. You just need to be pointed in the right direction. We have Turlingham to thank for that.'

'I'll kill him,' said Vic.

'No, you won't. Though if it's any consolation I'll see to that myself before the week is out. The man's a buffoon, but he knows where the bodies are buried, as they say. So let's get on with it, shall we? First, I'm going to finish opening this bottle, and then... I'm afraid the next part might take some time, since the blade is so small, and your waist is so very thick, and I don't possess Mordecai's supernatural strength... Then I'll replace what I've drunk with *your* vital juices. See these empty bottles? Those are for you. I'll stopper them up, eventually decant the contents into other vessels, maybe carbon fibre this time, whatever's most durable, and then in another five hundred years it'll be ready for me to drink. And that, my friend, is the cycle of the Half Man.'

'You're fucking delusional. Worse than French. At least he was a demon. What's your excuse?'

'Mordecai is a hedonist,' said Ridley, who seemed strangely anxious to earn Vic's approval. 'Out for no-one but himself. I'm doing this for the benefit of all mankind.'

'That makes me feel *so much* better,' said Vic.

Ridley picked up the bottle and resumed his battle with the corkscrew.

'Damn thing's jammed in too tight... French's mistake was to forget that I was around to stop him. But there's no-one left to stop *me*.'

He tugged at the cork again. There was a deep sucking sound, and it finally eased out of the neck with a dull pop which echoed round the cellar.

The air was filled with orgasmic sighing. Vic twisted his head from side to side, trying to see what was going on. The cellar seemed to be pressing in on him, the walls creeping closer.

Ridley brought the open bottle up to his nose and breathed in the bouquet, eyelids flickering in an expression of oenophiliac rapture. Vic waited for him to slurp it down, but instead the doctor set the bottle back down, next to the empties.

'We'll just let this breathe,' he said, picking up the machete.

'You fucking snob!' said Vic. He saw Ridley wince, and decided the least he could do before he died was insult his executioner as much as possible. He raised his head, preparing to let fly with another curse...

And spotted a dark figure in the shadows between the racks. A woman. Had she been there all the time?

'Help!' shouted Vic.

Ridley shook his head. 'I told you, Vic. There's no-one left but me and you.'

'Help!' Vic shouted again, straining at his bonds. 'This bastard wants to chop me in half! Help!'

His cries were so heartfelt that Ridley felt compelled to check behind him. He looked straight at Mrs. Rock. But didn't see her.

'Afraid you're on your own,' said Ridley.

Mrs. Rock moved forward until she was level with Ridley. She didn't appear to have noticed the machete.

'Mrs. Rock!' shouted Vic. 'Watch out! He's got a blade!'

Ridley frowned. 'What are you babbling about now? Who's Mrs. Rock?'

'Mr. Rock's wife. Who the hell do you think?'

Ridley glared at him impatiently. 'Rock doesn't have a wife.'

'Oh yes he does,' said Vic, feeling as though he were caught up in an absurd pantomime.

'He's a widower, you clod. Nasty piece of work. Beat her to death years ago, got off on a technicality.'

Vic was already cold, but now he felt himself go colder. If Rock's wife was dead, that meant...

'Well, I'm looking at her now.'

He stared up at the woman, realising there had always been something odd about her. Had he ever seen her speaking to anyone else? Hadn't she swept the floor, and served him breakfast? Her dark clothes merged with the shadows, but her face stood out pale, pale as death, in fact. Had it always been that pale? Vic couldn't remember.

There was an otherwordly groaning all around them, as though The Half Man were coming to life, with the two men trapped in its belly. Ridley glanced around again, slightly unnerved. But swallowed his misgivings and reached again for the precious bottle...

Which glided out of his grasp.

Ridley gasped in shock.

He couldn't see what Vic was seeing. Mrs. Rock had picked up the bottle. With her other hand, she gently worked the machete out of the doctor's grasp, took a step towards the slab, and raised it. It swished down and for a horrible moment Vic thought it was going to embed itself in his abdomen, but instead the blade sliced through the bonds around his wrists and ankles. Vic sat up, rubbing the circulation back into his hands.

Mrs. Rock looked at him intently, as if weighing her options. Then offered him the bottle.

Ridley made a strangled noise in his throat as he saw the bottle floating, as if by magic, into Vic's hands. He made a grab for it, but too late. Vic was already on his feet, dangling the prize at arm's length.

'One step nearer, you quack, and I'll drop it!'

'But it's the last one!' cried Ridley.

Vic looked from Ridley to Mrs. Rock, and than back at Ridley again.

'Hard cheese,' he said, and raised the bottle over his head, as if about to dash it on to the flagstone floor.

'NOOOOO!' shrieked Ridley.

Vic paused.

Plenty to drink here. Grab it while you can.

'On second thoughts,' he said, 'I *am* parched, and would be a shame to let this go to waste. Here's to the memory of Brian Curtis, intrepid anorak and unsung hero, even if he was a freaking nutter. And to Noreen Duval, snakewoman extraordinaire. Bottoms up, matey!'

He brought the bottle to his lips, tilted his head back, and poured the contents into his mouth.

The dead weight of history and the souls of a thousand victims hovered expectantly over the moment. The unnatural silence was punctuated only by the faint tinkling of ghostly wind chimes and the soft glugging as Vic necked the liquid.

Fortunately for him, it didn't taste like blood. It didn't taste like wine either. It tasted like ambrosia, and it was exactly what he needed. He really had been *very* thirsty. It seemed like several lifetimes ago that French had offered to buy him a drink before sucker-punching him in the face. But this! This had been worth the wait. He drained the bottle and let out a rich belch of satisfaction, wiping his mouth with the back of his hand.

'Best bloody liquor I ever tasted.'

Ridley's face contorted with rage. 'You're going to wish you'd never been born.'

He hurled himself at Vic, hands hooked into claws, ready to rip his throat out. Vic, in a reflex born of his South London acumen - now mixed with the effect of whatever it was he'd just drunk - calmly stepped aside and smashed the empty bottle over Ridley's head.

The doctor crumpled, but before he could hit the floor, Mrs. Rock caught him by the armpits and pushed him back on to the slab. Ridley lay there in a daze, staring up into her face.

'Ah, I can see her now.'

'I've been here all along,' said Mrs. Rock. 'You just didn't know how to look. Your kind never does.'

Understanding dawned in Ridley's startled eyes.

'You're Saxby's guardian.'

Mrs. Rock smiled down at him. 'The very same.'

'The old dog,' said Ridley. 'He was smarter than I thought.'

'Araminta's smart too,' said Mrs. Rock. 'I'll call her in the morning, let her know how things turned out. They're good people, the Saxbys. Unlike you, Ridley.'

'You have no idea what you've done!' shouted Ridley. 'Pearce is filthy lowlife! Ignorant scum!'

Mrs. Rock looked over at Vic, who was crooning to himself.

And I will drink your blood like wine
And your bones will decompose

'We'll see,' said Mrs. Rock. 'People can change.'

In the marshlands of the east
Where the samphire grows

'Oh, shut up!' said Ridley. *'Shut up!'*

Mrs. Rock started to unbutton his shirt. He tried to stop her, but she pushed him back easily, securing his wrists with a flick of her hand.

'What are you doing, you witch?'

She finished opening his shirt and picked up the machete. 'Keeping a well-stocked cellar.'

Ridley's eyes opened wide. 'You can't do that. It was supposed to be Pearce. It was always going to be Pearce!'

'But doctor,' said Mrs. Rock. 'You too are qualified, are you not? You've been marked with the sign of the snake, and we all know there have been plenty of blood rituals. That unpleasantness in Prague, for example.'

'Steele was asking for it!' shouted Ridley. 'He was a common thief!'

'I'm not talking about Steele,' said Mrs. Rock. 'You're lucky Castle Pretorius was razed to the ground after the war, and all the evidence with it.'

'Research!' shouted Ridley. 'It helped make me the man I am today!'

'Exactly,' said Mrs. Rock.

There was a rumbling from the cellar walls. Mrs. Rock looked directly at Vic. Only now did he see how lifeless her eyes were. But they weren't evil, just dead.

'You should go,' she said.

Vic strolled towards the stairs as though he had all the time in the world, then stopped and looked back at her. 'What about you?'

Mrs. Rock smiled, a little sadly. 'I can never leave.'

'Suit yourself.' Vic shrugged and walked on.

Mrs. Rock called after him. 'Don't let it go to your head, Mr. Pearce! Choose wisely!'

*****

Shafts of moonlight filtered through the boarded-up windows as Vic padded barefoot across the bar. He was bare-chested and shivering, and the only garment he could find was a torn T-shirt with a picture of a Nazi sodomising a cowboy. Still, it was better than nothing, and there was no left to mock him, so he slipped it over his head. In the taproom he found a pair of winklepickers and squeezed his frozen feet into them before helping himself to a cigarette from a packet someone had left on the bar. On second thoughts, he pocketed the whole packet, since there was no-one left to smoke it but him. He was the last man standing. He lit the cigarette and walked towards the remains of the front door, relieved to see no trace of Mr. Rock's corpse. He wondered if Ridley had cleared it up, or had used one of his stupid magician's tricks to make it vanish. Either way, it was gone, and Vic was thankful for that. He'd seen enough corpses to last him a lifetime.

As he stepped over the threshold into the night, there was a bloodcurdling scream from the cellar. Vic tried not to flinch, and walked on.

Outside, the wind still had a bitter edge, but the weather was settling now, the night sky calmer. Vic tilted his face up to the moon, relishing its silvery glow. He felt different. All sorts of thoughts were racing through his head - some of them, he suspected, not his own. He'd led a life that some folk might have described as wicked, but maybe he could put that behind him. Maybe he *could* be a better person. As Mrs. Rock had said, he just had to make the right choices.

More hideous screaming, fainter now, as he slid into the driver's seat of Griff's red Alfa Romeo.

The screaming stopped.

Vic paused to savour his freedom, looking around at the wrecked cars. Boy, that had been a narrow escape. If it hadn't been for Mrs. Rock, it might have been him screaming down there...

Something about the cars was different.

No sooner had he clocked the Jaguar parked next to the deformed Mercedes than he felt the muzzle of a sawn-off shotgun pressing against his head, just above his left ear. It wasn't hard to guess whose finger was on the trigger.

'Hello, Mr. Turlingham,' he said.

He'd always known Little Jimmy would catch up with him eventually, though he was surprised the old man had dragged himself all the way up here instead of sending another of his lackeys.

He was also surprised to note that he didn't feel in the least bit worried about it.

'What the fuck you wearing?' said Turlingham. 'You a fag now?'

Vic looked down at his T-shirt. 'Something I picked up.'

'Thought you'd done a runner, Vic. What you been up to?'

'Just having a drink.'

'And Saxby's treasure? Did you get it?'

'I did,' said Vic.

'Well?'

Vic patted his stomach. 'It was very tasty.'

Turlingham's jaw dropped. 'The fuck? You swallowed it? It's *inside* you?'

'Safe a place as any.'

Turlingham's face hardened into granite. 'So I have to wait till you shit it out? On second thoughts, I'm a busy man. I'll cut it out of you with a straight razor.'

'Reminds me,' said Vic. 'Spoken to Thin Tony recently?'

'Fallen off the map,' said Turlingham. 'Just like you're going to fall off it, Vic. And then I'll throw the Saxby bitch after you.'

'I can take you round to Saxby Hall right now, if you like,' said Vic. 'Was thinking of popping in to see her anyway, before I drive back to London. I've a feeling she can give me some useful advice. Hop in.' He patted the passenger seat.

'Shut it, Pearce.'

Turlingham cocked the trigger.

'Wouldn't do that if I were you,' said Vic.

'Well you're not me, are you. And I've had enough of your lip.'

'And I've had enough of yours,' said Vic, turning his head away at the very instant that Turlingham fired.

There was no way Little Jimmy could have missed, not at that range. Yet miss he did. The slug tore past Vic's ear, ricocheted off the dashboard and struck Turlingham in the chest, knocking him backwards. The shotgun flew out of his grasp. The fat man sat up, disbelief written all over his face, his fingers groping for the wound, trying to stem the blood.

'The fuck?' he shouted. 'You fucker, Pearce! I'll get you for this!'

Vic thought about getting out of the car, retrieving the shotgun and putting one through Little Jimmy's head, but it seemed like too much trouble, and besides, hadn't he just decided he was going to turn a new leaf? The idea of mending his ways tickled him.

'Get to a hospital, they should be able to fix you up,' he said, flicking his cigarette at Turlingham. 'Was a sawbones right here till a moment ago, but afraid you just missed him.' He bent forward again, pinched the wires together and the Alfa Romeo coughed into life.

'See you, Jimmy.' He set off down the track, humming as he drove. He felt like a new man, older but wiser, more confident, and only slightly drunk. And surprisingly chipper, considering all he'd been through.

196

After a couple of hundred yards, he glanced in the rearview mirror, expecting to catch one last glimpse of The Half Man. One for the road, as it were.

What he saw made him stamp on the brake and swivel in his seat to get a better look.

The Half Man stood on the horizon, but it had changed. No longer was it the creepy old inn where he'd just spent the worst night of his life. Now it was a rotting shell with crumbling walls and windows empty like dead eyes.

Nothing could possibly have lived in a ruin like that, let alone served him pints of Black Monk and a Full English Breakfast.

A sinister creaking echoed around the moonlit marshes.

In front of the ruin, Mrs. Rock was winching the top half of Ridley's corpse so that it dangled from the gibbet-like inn sign, entrails streaming in the breeze.

Vic grimaced and turned his back on the grisly sight. Christ, he needed a smoke. He reached into his pocket for the cigarette packet... And his fingers closed on something cold and hard and smooth. He drew the object out and stared at it: a gold anklet shaped like a snake. He had no idea how it had got there.

He had a feeling he hadn't seen the last of Noreen Duval. But it wasn't a bad feeling.

'Yeah,' he said. 'Bottoms up.'

He grinned, gunned the engine, and drove off through the receding floods towards the rest of what promised to be an exceedingly long and extremely eventful life.

THE END

AUTHOR'S NOTE

The Half Man began life as a screenplay I co-wrote in 1996 with Lawrence Jackson.

Twenty years later, I approached our screenplay as a plot outline and reworked it as a novel. I suppose this would technically make it a novelisation, although I never considered it as such while writing it.

Nevertheless, the characters, plot and setting owe as much to Mr. Jackson's imagination as to mine. I hereby dedicate this book to him.

ABOUT THE AUTHOR

Anne Billson is a film critic, novelist, photographer, screenwriter and international cat-sitter. She has lived in London, Tokyo, Cambridge, Paris and Croydon, and now lives in Belgium. She likes frites, beer and chocolate.

Her books include horror novels *Suckers*, *Stiff Lips*, *The Ex* and *The Coming Thing*, as well as *Cats on Film*, monographs on John Carpenter's film *The Thing* and Tomas Alfredson's *Let the Right One In*, and *Billson Film Database*, a collection of film reviews.

In 1993 she was named one of Granta's 'Best Young British Novelists'. From 1992 to 2001 she was film critic of the *Sunday Telegraph*.

She has three blogs:

Multiglom (the Billson blog)

Cats on Film (a blog about films that have cats in them)

L'empire des lumières (a blog about Belgium)

She can be contacted on Twitter at @AnneBillson

SUCKERS

'Billson honours the rules of the genre, then proceeds to have fun with them... Dark, sharp, chic and very funny' (Christopher Fowler - *Time Out*)

'A superb satirist' (Salman Rushdie)

'Merits a post position on everybody's reading list, even those who don't usually like vampire stories. It isn't splatter fiction; it's an honest piece of literature' (Elliott Swanson - *Booklist*)

'A black and bloody celebration of wit, womanhood and slapstick, beautifully sustained to a thoroughly satisfying climax' (Chris Gilmore - *Interzone*)

'A very camp and hugely entertaining vampire novel' (Christie Hickman - *Midweek*)

'Wicked and vulgar and unsettling... rollicking knockabout gore... nasty and brutishly funny' (Patt Morrison - *Los Angeles Times*)

'Enchanting and ominous at the same time; a rare and impressive piece of literary juggling' (Jonathan Carroll)

'A distinctive, original and refreshing debut' (Kim Newman - *Starburst*)

STIFF LIPS

'A slick and remarkably controlled performance which more than equals her satisfying first novel *Suckers*. Ghost tales invariably leave me cold. I read this one in a single highly enjoyable sitting' (Paul Rutman - *Sunday Telegraph*)

'With *Stiff Lips*, Billson overturns the clichés of the horror genre, establishing, in their stead, her own original voice' (Lucy O'Brien - *The Independent*)

'Sexy, sardonic and distinctly spooky... a tale to make you shiver - if you don't die laughing first' (*Cosmopolitan*)

'*Stiff Lips* achieves an authentic and unsettling nastiness' (*Sunday Times*)

'A vastly entertaining story... As well as being a successful ghost story, *Stiff Lips* is an amusing satire... Funny and spooky - an excellent combination' (Sophia Watson - *The Spectator*)

'An absolutely terrific ghost story, taut and well-written with vivid characters and a spot-on blackly comic/satirical vein that does not detract from the very effective horror' (Lynda Rucker)

'Very creepy, thoroughly modern ghost story about frenemies, real-estate envy, going-for-the-gold bitchery and what makes the perfect boyfriend' (Maitland McDonagh)

'An engagingly creepy story of status anxiety in Notting Hill, where one flat appears to be stuck in a macabre capsule of its own sordid past amid the surrounding gentrification. As in *Suckers* the tale revolves an insecure ugly duckling heroine on the fringes of an effortlessly entitled social set, the dramas of London's property bubble and a generous dose of the supernatural macabre, and it is Billson's great strength as a writer that the horror elements fit seamlessly into her world. It works as a ghost story and a social satire, and succeeds in making these apparently incongruous ingredients taste better together'
(D. Small)

THE EX

'Great wit, great dialogue, great scares, genuinely disturbing yet never less than thoroughly entertaining, this book is a terrific read' (Stephen Volk)

'Witty, blackly comic, pacy and original. Seedy anti-hero John Croydon is the supernatural version of Len Deighton's Harry Palmer. Or as if Harold Lloyd had strayed into *The Omen*. Slapstick as well as chills. It moves expertly from set-piece to set-piece in locations both grubby and glamorous. Totally recommended' (Lawrence Jackson)

'a fast paced, supernatural detective novel with a welcome vein of black humour running through it' (Oliver Clarke)

'Another page-turning spine-chiller from the author of *Suckers*... contains Billson's usual mix of dark humour, social satire and imaginative creepiness (Simon Litton)

Another winner from Anne Billson. Horror and humour in equal measure... The story itself is like a cross between M. R. James and Raymond Chandler with our hero employed to protect a prospective bride from her fiancés 'ex' who just happens to be dead... But as the story moves from urban London to an Hammeresque rural setting the story takes another turn involving a family curse. Readers familiar with Anne Billson's previous horror novels will not be disappointed. Laughs and scares come thick and fast and the whole thing speeds along like a vintage Rolls Royce. I couldn't recommend this highly enough and any book that references Robert Aickman and Ronnie James Dio is a must buy surely!' (R.T. Brown)

'another clever, creepy, wickedly funny book from Anne Billson, a great follow-up to *Suckers* and *Stiff Lips* (not a sequel, though there are references to events and characters from *Stiff Lips*). This time she tackles a ghost story with a male protagonist, a fairly hapless private investigator who has been hired to protect Alice, a bride-to-be who thinks she is being stalked by her fiancé's ex-wife Georgina - who happens to be dead... Billson includes many 'easter-egg' nods and references to well-known ghost stories and films (she knows her stuff), and leads you a merry dance, keeping you guessing as to who or what has it in for Alice. The situations may often be comical... but these are more than balanced out by the scary set-pieces (more difficult than you'd think - too often comedy-horror fails to work on one or both levels), and I found myself caring far more about the fate of the main characters than I initially expected. A thoroughly entertaining read, jolly good fun' (Esther Sherman)

THE COMING THING

'How to describe *The Coming Thing*? *Rosemary's Baby* directed by Howard Hawks with a touch of *The Producers*? To be honest that probably doesn't do this novel justice. It is one of the most original horror novels I've read in a very long time. It is also one of the funniest' (R. T. Brown)

'Nancy is an unsuccessful London actress whose life goes decidedly pear-shaped when she gets pregnant - with the Antichrist. Anne Billson's *The Coming Thing* is a hell of a romp. It's like an inventive, witty and fast-moving cocktail of Ealing Comedy, the *Final Destination* films, *The Plank*, '80s satire, and more' (Braz)

'Irresistibly engaging, witty, and gruesome. The perfect treat for the intelligent horror fan, *The Coming Thing* bounces along briskly, but just beneath the surface one glimpses Big Dark Themes, like the shadows of huge fish beneath a sparkling ocean'

'An entertaining romp full of jokes, action, scares and social commentary. The tone is a little more outrageous this time, compared to the understated chills of her previous novel *The Ex*, with lashings of gore and a wild plot stuffed with a weird supporting cast. What grounds it and makes it more than satisfying is the attention paid to developing convincing and interesting characters. Billson's protagonists are always unusual, often misfits or outsiders but not in a clichéd or predictable way, and their believable sets of quirks and neuroses, even occasionally bordering on unlikeability, is refreshing' (S. Litton)

'*The Coming Thing*, about the impending birth of the Antichrist (in pre-millennial London!) is so funny and more than a bit freaky. It manages to navigate the line between horror and comedy effortlessly. Imagine if Clive Barker had made *Notting Hill*, or if you threw both *Rosemary's Baby* and *Bridget Jones's Baby* into a literary playpen! Very much recommended as a hilarious and spooky page-turner.'

Printed in Great Britain
by Amazon